A Knotty Problem

Book 7 in **The Math Kids** Series

The Math Kids Series
Have you read them all?

1. The Prime-Time Burglars
2. A Sequence of Events
3. An Unusual Pattern
4. An Encrypted Clue
5. An Incorrect Solution
6. The Triangle Secret

A Knotty Problem

Book 7 in **The Math Kids** Series

by
David Cole

Common Deer Press

Published by Common Deer Press Incorporated

Text Copyright © 2022 David Cole
Illustration Copyright © Shannon O'Toole

All rights reserved under International and Pan-American Copyright conventions. No part of this book may be reproduced in any form or by any electronic or mechanical means, including information storage and retrieval systems, without permission in writing from the publisher, except by a reviewer, who may quote brief passages in a review.

Published in 2022 by Common Deer Press
1745 Rockland Avenue
Victoria, British Columbia
V8S 1W6

This book is a work of fiction. Names, characters, places, and incidents are either the product of the author's imagination or are used fictitiously.

Library and Archives Canada Cataloguing in Publication

Title: The triangle secret / by David Cole.
Names: Cole, David, 1957- author.
Series: Cole, David, 1957- Math kids ; 6.
Description: Series statement: The math kids series ; book 6
Identifiers: Canadiana 20210371404
| ISBN 9781988761626 (softcover)
Classification: LCC PZ7.1.C64 Tri 2022 | DDC j813/.6—dc23

Cover Image: Shannon O'Toole
Book Design: David Moratto

Printed in Canada
www.CommonDeerPress.com

*To Maude Carmichael,
who inspired my love of math
in the third grade.*

Prologue

The sleek blue helicopter swooped in low over the top of McNair Elementary School. From the helicopter's window, Jordan Waters could clearly see a partially deflated volleyball near one edge of the roof.

"Do you see that?" he asked.

"Yeah, I bet that's the one Dylan kicked up there during recess last week," Justin Grant said.

Jordan started to ask if the pilot could land on the roof so they could retrieve the ball but thought better about it.

"Is that Vivie and Ally on the playground?" Catherine Duchesne asked. The two sisters were twins and never went anywhere without the other.

"I think so," Stephanie Lewis said. She waved her hand frantically as the two girls looked up. The twins waved back and stared as the helicopter settled gently onto the grassy soccer field.

"Thanks so much for the helicopter ride!" Jordan said enthusiastically with an ear-to-ear grin on his face.

"Don't mention it, Jordan," Willard Howell said with a smile almost as wide. "It was the least I could do."

The four friends had helped the eccentric billionaire out of a tricky situation. To return the favor, Howell had agreed to grant Jordan's wish of a ride in his helicopter.

Once the rotors had spun down, Howell hopped out of the helicopter and helped the four to the ground.

"You're okay making it home from here?" he asked.

"Sure, Mr. Howell," Justin answered. "It's only a couple of blocks."

"Well, I want to thank each of you again," he said, solemnly shaking each of their hands. "You know I still owe you one, right?"

"We'll keep that in mind, Mr. Howell," Jordan said.

"I mean it. I'm only a phone call away," Howell said. He glanced down at his watch. "I've got to get going now. Thanks again!"

Howell climbed back into the helicopter. The pilot waited until the kids were a safe distance away before spinning up the rotors. The helicopter rose gracefully in the air, pivoted into the wind, and then sped away. The four stared after it until it was just a blue speck in the distance.

"Is that your helicopter?" Vivie asked. She and her sister had come up behind them as the helicopter flew away.

Stephanie laughed. "No, Ally, that's not ours."

"I'm Vivie."

A Knotty Problem

"Are you sure?" Stephanie asked. She was convinced she had finally figured out how to tell the twins apart.

"I'm pretty sure," Vivie said.

"Yeah," Ally added, "she's definitely Vivie."

"Sorry about that," Stephanie said.

"It's okay. It happens all the time," Ally said. "Even our parents get it wrong sometimes."

"Are you sure that's not your helicopter?" Vivie asked again.

"I'm afraid not," Jordan said. "Maybe someday, but not today."

"If you ever get one, will you take us for a ride?" Ally asked.

"Sure," Jordan answered.

"Okay," Ally said. "We've got to go." She and her sister turned and walked away.

"I've got to get home myself," Justin said.

"Me too," Stephanie agreed.

"Okay, but we're still meeting on Saturday after Stephanie's soccer game, right?" Jordan asked. "The district math competition is coming up and we need to be prepared."

"Oh, we'll be ready," Catherine said. "Nothing can stand in our way this year."

She smiled, not knowing their team and their very friendships would soon be tested to the breaking point.

Chapter 1

Stephanie used her right foot to settle a sharp cross field pass from Riley Clark, quickly shifted the soccer ball to her left foot to keep it away from the nearest defender, then drilled a shot into the upper left-hand corner of the goal. She smiled as she heard a squeal of delight from the sideline. She recognized the voice of Catherine, her best friend, and gave a small nod of recognition in her direction.

"Great shot, Stephanie!" Riley said as she caught up to her teammate. The two exchanged a high five.

"It wouldn't have happened without your amazing pass," Stephanie replied.

"True," Riley said. "That was an amazing pass."

Stephanie grinned and put an arm over Riley's shoulders as they walked toward midfield. "The only thing more amazing than that pass is your modesty."

Riley nodded solemnly. "You're right, Stephanie. When you get past my incredible soccer skills, good looks, and

A Knotty Problem

great sense of humor, I think it's my modesty that really stands out."

Stephanie burst into laughter while Riley tried to keep a straight face.

"You two want to join us?" the ref called out.

"Oh, sorry!" Stephanie yelled and hustled to midfield for the kickoff.

Two minutes later, the ref blew his whistle to signal the end of the game. Stephanie glanced over at the scoreboard. Her team had won eight to zero in a game that saw her score four times and assist on two other goals. Her teammates swarmed around her as she walked off the field.

"Great game, Stephanie!"

"Way to go, Steph!"

"Amazing game, Stephanie!"

Her face turned a bright red in embarrassment. She shrugged her shoulders in response to the compliments.

"Good game, Stephanie," said Logan Clark, her coach and Riley's dad. "I hope you saved some of that fancy footwork for the state tournament."

"It was a great team effort," Stephanie said.

"Like my amazing pass," Riley chimed in, drawing a look from her dad which quickly turned to a grin as he saw her earnest expression.

"There's not much to talk about," the coach addressed

the team. "Great passing, and a lot of good shots. Let's hear it for the offense."

The girls all applauded and several clapped Stephanie on the back.

"And let's not forget the defense. Shutting out a good team like this isn't easy. Good job of sticking to your opponents and clogging up the passing lanes. Let's hear it for the defense."

The team clapped again.

"And finally, let's not forget about a couple of really nice saves by Sydney!"

Sydney Maine took a dramatic deep bow while her teammates cheered.

"So a great game across the board," Coach Clark said. "I guess you already know, but this win assures us a spot in the state tournament. Pick up one of the packets with all the details and make sure it gets into your parents' hands. Okay, that does it for me. Get out of here and enjoy the rest of your weekend."

Stephanie gathered her stuff and walked over to where Catherine was folding up her lawn chair.

"Great game, Stephanie!" Catherine said. "That last goal happened so fast I almost missed it."

"It was fun. That may have been one of the best games I've ever played," Stephanie admitted. "I hope I can play that well in the state tournament."

A Knotty Problem

She glanced down at the stack of papers in her hands. The color drained from her face.

"What's wrong?" asked Catherine with concern.

"It's the tournament."

"What about it?"

"It's on the same weekend as the district math tournament," Stephanie said.

"Oh, no! Are you sure?"

Stephanie handed the papers to Catherine. Her friend's face fell as she confirmed the date.

"Justin is going to go through the roof," Stephanie said. "All that work we've done is going to be wasted."

The Math Kids had won the school math contest in fourth grade but lost in the finals of the district competition. When they advanced from fourth to fifth grade, they found that Mr. Miller, their new teacher, hated math. But after the four helped keep Mr. Miller's son from going to jail, he had allowed them to form their own math group to continue working toward avenging their loss in the district math competition.

Now all the studying, all the weekends working on increasingly difficult math problems, all the dreams of holding up that trophy looked like they were all for nothing.

"You're right," Catherine said glumly, "Justin is going to go through the roof."

***

"You've got one to your left!" Justin cried out.

"Got him," Jordan replied. "You cover the right side and I'll move up along this ridge." He grimaced and scanned left and right as he inched his way forward.

"Incoming!"

There was a thunderous boom as an alien grenade blew up near Jordan's character. His health points went quickly to zero and Jordan dropped his controller in frustration.

"That's the third time I've fallen for that trap," he said. "It looks completely clear and then bam, I'm dead. Maybe next time I'll just plow right down the middle of the valley instead."

"Nah, you tried that too," Justin said. "Next time let's try hugging the right side and double-teaming the alien sentries."

Jordan and Justin both loved to play video games, although Justin was hands down the better of the two. Both Justin and Jordan got a weekly allowance for doing chores around their houses. While Jordan spent his money as soon as he received it, Justin carefully saved every cent until he had enough money to buy the latest game. This new one was the toughest they had played.

"I'm actually glad this one is going to take a while to beat," Justin said. "*Andromeda Attack* was way too easy."

A Knotty Problem

"You think maybe we should try an easier setting?" Jordan asked.

"No way," his best friend protested. "We can beat this, I know it."

"Okay, let's restart and give it another shot then."

"I've got a better idea," Justin said. "Let's take a break and tackle that problem Mr. Miller gave us."

"You don't want to wait for Stephanie and Catherine?"

"I think they're still at Stephanie's soccer game. We can at least get a start on it."

For Jordan and Justin, shooting aliens was one of the best ways to spend a Saturday afternoon. The other was solving math problems, the more difficult the better.

Justin dug into his overloaded backpack. Jordan watched in amusement as his friend pulled out three golf balls, a realistic rubber snake, four books, a handful of rubber bands, a roll of cellophane tape, and a pair of broken sunglasses before he finally retrieved a pile of papers.

"Why do you always have so much stuff in your backpack?" Jordan asked.

"I like to be prepared."

"Prepared for what?"

"Anything," Justin replied.

Jordan looked skeptical. "It looks like random junk to me."

"Random?" Justin asked. "No way. This is all carefully planned out."

"Okay, so what are the golf balls for?" Jordan asked.

"Defense against rabid animals," Justin replied. "You just peg the animal in the head, and it will take off."

"Why three balls?"

"I'm not that good a shot."

Jordan laughed. "Okay, and what about the snake?"

"That's easy," Justin replied. "That's to keep mice from sneaking into my pack to eat the snacks I have hidden down at the bottom."

"Why do you need the sunglasses?"

"In case it gets sunny."

"But they're broken."

"That's why I have the tape and rubber bands to hold them together."

"Okay, I give up," Jordan said. "This is all important stuff."

"You bet it is," Justin said. "And now, here's the math problem Mr. Miller gave us." He pulled a single crumpled sheet from the stack of papers and placed it on the coffee table.

The doorbell rang. Justin looked annoyed as he went to answer the door. When he returned with Stephanie and Catherine, Jordan was carefully studying the problem.

"Hey guys," he said. "This problem looks pretty easy. It's a lot like the sixes problem Mrs. Gouche gave us last year! This will be a breeze to solve."

A Knotty Problem

"Cool," Stephanie said.

"How was your soccer game?" Jordan asked. "You win?"

"Of course they did," Catherine said. "And Stephanie had half of the goals!"

"Nice," Jordan said.

"That was your last game, wasn't it?" Justin asked.

"Yeah," Stephanie said. "Except for..." Her voice trailed off as she thought about what would come next.

"Except for what?" Jordan prompted.

Stephanie exchanged a long glance with Catherine. It did not go unnoticed by Justin.

"What is it you're not telling us?" he asked.

Stephanie took a deep breath and then told them about the conflict between the soccer tournament and the math competition. Her prediction about Justin's reaction was right on the money—he went through the roof.

"You can't miss the math competition!" he exclaimed.

"I don't think I have any choice," Stephanie said. "It's the state tournament."

"And it's the district math competition. We have to avenge our loss from last year."

"But it's the first time our team has made it to state," Stephanie said. "The team needs me."

"What about our team?" Justin asked. "You can't drop

11

out just when we need you most. You joined the Math Kids, so you have a duty to do everything you can to support the team. That's all there is to it."

"No, it isn't," Stephanie said. "You're forgetting that I have another team that's also counting on me."

"But there are only four of us," Justin countered. "Your soccer team has lots of other players."

"Stephanie is the best player on the team," Catherine said. "If she doesn't play in the state tournament, they'll probably lose. They need her."

"Well, we need her too!" Justin shot back. "We'll definitely lose without her."

"Hey, I'm not happy about this either," Stephanie said. "You know I want to be in the math competition."

"Then do it," Justin said.

"But I also want to play in the state soccer tournament."

"I guess you'll have to make a decision then," Justin said, his voice eerily calm. "Either you're a part of the Math Kids or you're not."

Stephanie's eyes opened wide in surprise at his statement. "Are you saying I can't be in the Math Kids if I don't go to the district competition?"

"That's what I'm saying," Justin said firmly.

"I guess that means I'm out then," she said.

"Fine. Have it your way," Justin replied.

Catherine looked at Jordan, hoping he would step in to help, but he looked as helpless as she felt.

A Knotty Problem

"Look, guys," Catherine said. "Can't we talk about this?"

"What's there to talk about?" Justin asked. "Stephanie is choosing her stupid soccer team over us."

"It's not stupid!" Stephanie shot back.

"Catherine's right," Jordan finally chimed in. "Isn't there some way we can figure this out?"

"It's simple," Justin said. "If she's out of the math competition, she's out of the group."

Catherine's face became red with anger. "Well, if Stephanie is out, I'm out too."

"That's your choice."

Catherine stared at Justin, who stared right back. Jordan didn't know how to respond. He was watching their close group of friends break up right in front of his eyes.

"Hey, c'mon guys," he started, trying to figure out some way to ease the tension.

Stephanie was having none of it. She turned on her heel and left. Catherine followed her out of the room, out of Justin's house, and out of the Math Kids.

"We have to do something," Jordan said, almost pleading with Justin.

"No, we don't. They made their choice, and they have to live with it. Now, how about tackling that math problem since we won't be getting any help from Stephanie and Catherine?"

Chapter 2

The next morning, Stephanie was still angry about her encounter with Justin the previous day. *How dare he kick me out of the Math Kids? It wouldn't have even been started without me.* She decided to go for a run to reduce her frustration.

She grabbed her earbuds from the top of her desk and was annoyed to see they were twisted into knots. She spent the next few minutes untangling them and trying to figure out how they had become knotted. As an only child, she didn't have any siblings to blame for messing with her stuff, but she was sure they hadn't been tangled when she last used them.

She plugged the earbuds into her phone and picked an upbeat music mix to play while she ran. After a quick stretch, she left the house, turning right toward the park. She started at a slow jog to loosen up her legs, then accelerated as she got closer to the park, her long legs eating up the distance. As she turned into the entrance, she sped up even more. When she reached the edge of the soccer field, she broke into an all-out sprint, running as hard as she could for the length of the field, head down and arms pumping rhythmically as her heart pounded in her chest. Passing the goal, she slowed to a run and then back to a jog as she turned back toward home.

As she ran, she couldn't help but continue to think about Justin's reaction to her missing the math competition. On the one hand, she understood his disappointment. *What he doesn't understand is that I'm disappointed too,* she thought. On the other hand, she also had to think about her soccer teammates. *This is the first time our soccer team has made it to the state championship, and I can't let them down now. Life is full of choices, and this is one I had to make.*

She just wished Justin could understand her decision.

***

Jordan picked at his breakfast, stirring his cereal around in the bowl. He was frustrated. He had watched his best friendships fall apart right before his very eyes, and he had done nothing to stop it. Now he was replaying everything in his head, trying to figure out what he could have done differently.

The situation was difficult because he could see both sides. He understood that Stephanie needed to play in her soccer tournament. If she didn't, she would be letting

A Knotty Problem

down her team. He also understood how Justin felt about Stephanie choosing her soccer teammates over her Math Kids teammates. It wasn't fair to work so hard and then have someone leave the team just when they were needed most.

"I heard your girlfriend broke up with you," his sister Linda taunted from across the table. Linda was three years older and loved to tease her little brother. Jordan tried to kick her but only succeeded in slamming his toe against the wooden table leg. He wanted to cry out in pain, but he knew his sister would only laugh.

"She's not my girlfriend," he snarled.

"She's a girl and your friend, so I'd say that makes her your girlfriend. I mean, I guess she *was* your girlfriend until she broke up with you."

"She didn't break up with me!"

"Oh, so she's still your girlfriend?" Linda teased.

"She's not my girlfriend!" Jordan shouted back.

"You sure spend a lot of time with her if she's not," Linda said.

"And you spend almost all your time with Roger," Jordan shot back. "I guess that makes him your boyfriend."

"As a matter of fact, it does," Linda replied with a smile.

"Well, Stephanie is not my girlfriend," Jordan said quietly.

"So why did she break up with you?"

"She didn't break up with me!"

"Oh, you broke up with her?" Linda asked.

"No one broke up with anyone!" Jordan abruptly rose from his chair, knocking his bowl of cereal over and spilling milk everywhere. Linda laughed gleefully, knowing that she had really gotten under his skin this time.

Jordan sloppily wiped up the mess from the table and took his dripping bowl to the counter, drops of milk marking his path across the floor. He knew his mom would probably yell at him later, but right now all he wanted to do was to get away from his sister. He went to his room and closed and locked the door behind him. He flopped onto his bed and stared morosely at the ceiling. The same thought played over and over in his head: Their team was breaking up. What could he do to fix this mess?

They'd come so far since he, Justin, and Stephanie had formed the Math Kids in fourth grade. They'd solved all kinds of math problems in class, but they'd also used their skills to solve real-life problems too. When a string of burglaries hit the neighborhood, the three friends had figured out how to track the next target for the burglars. They had alerted the police and caught the criminals in the act.

When they'd needed a fourth person to join their team for the school math competition, they had chosen Catherine. But just before the contest, Catherine's father, a math professor at the college, had been kidnapped. He

A Knotty Problem

had managed to get a secret message to his daughter, and the four friends had figured out the clues and were able to rescue him and capture the kidnappers. That had introduced them to FBI Special Agent Bob Carlson, who had later enlisted their help in solving cases involving an old bank robbery and the strange will left by Willard Howell.

And then there was the time when Stephanie had found a cipher scribbled in an old book about their town of Maynard. The four of them had decrypted a secret message that led them to a fortune in gold under an old mansion overlooking the town. Without their discovery, there wouldn't even be a math competition this year. Now, with the Math Kids reduced to just Jordan and Justin, would they have any real shot at winning?

But was it really about winning? Thinking back on all of their adventures, Jordan realized he had come to rely on the strong bond that had developed between the four friends. They depended on each other and, up until now, they had always been there for each other. Was that why Justin was so mad about Stephanie choosing her soccer tournament over the math competition? Did he feel threatened that Stephanie didn't take the Math Kids as seriously as he did?

***

"Dad, do you have a few minutes to talk?" Catherine asked.

"I always have time for you," her dad answered, putting the newspaper down so he could give her his full attention.

"I have a little bit of a problem."

Her dad's forehead wrinkled. It was the same look he gave when he was concerned or thinking extra hard about a problem.

"Math problem?"

"No, this one is a people problem," she answered.

"Oh, those can be the worst," he said. "Math problems usually have a solution, or at least we can prove they don't have one. With people, though, it's not always clear."

"I know what you mean. This one is particularly tough."

"I take it this has something to do with the Math Kids?"

"You got that right. You see, Stephanie has this soccer tournament on the same weekend as the district math competition."

"Ouch," her dad said.

"Ouch is right. She has a really tough decision to make."

"And where do you fit into the problem?"

"Well, Stephanie is my best friend, and I think my job is to support her decision no matter what she decides," Catherine said.

A Knotty Problem

"Even if it's not the decision you would make?"

"No matter what," she said firmly.

Her dad smiled. "Then I think you've already solved your own problem," he said.

"That's only part of the problem."

He nodded. "I take it maybe the boys are not on board with her decision?"

As always, Catherine was amazed at how quickly her dad could get to the heart of the matter, whether it was math or people problems. "Justin is really mad about it. He said Stephanie either has to be in the math competition or she is out of the Math Kids."

"And how did Stephanie respond to that?" her dad asked.

"She quit."

"And you support her decision?"

"I do. In fact, I quit too." Tears welled up in her eyes. Her father reached over and took her hand.

"I know it feels bad right now, but if it's any consolation, I think you made the right decision."

"But it doesn't solve the problem," Catherine sobbed.

"Actually, I think it does."

"How? Everyone is mad at everyone else and there's no more Math Kids."

"I think it solves it because it was never your problem in the first place," her dad explained.

"I know it was Stephanie's problem, but—"

"No," her dad interrupted. "It was never Stephanie's problem either."

"Then whose problem is it?" Catherine asked.

"Think about it a little," he prompted.

Catherine thought for a moment. "Well, I guess it's a problem with the schedule."

"True, a person can't be in two places at the same time. Unfortunately, that's a problem that has no solution. I was thinking more about the people side of the problem."

Catherine thought a little more while her father sipped his hot tea. Whose problem was it really? It wasn't Stephanie's fault the tournament fell on the same weekend as the math competition. And it wasn't really Jordan's problem. He had at least tried to intervene, although she wished he had been a little more forceful in confronting Justin. It sure wasn't her own problem; she was only trying to support her best friend. Finally, she figured out what her dad was trying to get her to see. "It's Justin's problem, isn't it?"

He nodded. "I think you nailed it, Catherine. Stephanie had to make a tough choice and her teammate didn't support her. I think that makes the problem his, not yours."

"But how can I change his mind?" she asked.

"Now that is a different problem," he answered. "I think it might just take a little time, but he's a smart kid and I have a feeling he'll figure it out himself."

A Knotty Problem

***

Like his friends, Justin was troubled, but for a different reason. He just couldn't understand why everyone was mad at him. He wasn't the one who had chosen soccer over the Math Kids. All Stephanie had to do was change her mind, and everything would be back to normal.

He decided to play some video games to take his mind off his dilemma. He fired up his gaming system and spent the next thirty minutes mindlessly shooting alien invaders, the sounds of laser pistols and plasma grenades reverberating through the house.

"Hey Justin, can you turn the volume down for a few minutes?" his dad said from the doorway. "I'm expecting an important call."

"Sure," Justin said. He clicked mute on the TV remote.

"Thanks."

"Who's calling?" Justin asked.

"Oh, it's just a work thing," his dad answered.

"On a Sunday?"

His dad shrugged his shoulders as he walked away, his cell phone in one hand. A few minutes later, he heard his dad's familiar ringtone and his hearty greeting to someone named Phil. The door to his dad's home office clicked shut and Justin couldn't hear anything more, so he returned to his mission of ridding the planet of unwanted guests from outer space.

A Knotty Problem

His heart didn't seem to be in it though. He was worried about seeing everyone at school the next morning. Normally he loved going to school, especially on days where they had math groups, but he had a bad feeling things were not going to go well.

Chapter 3

Justin's premonition was right. Monday morning in class was about as uncomfortable as it could get. Catherine and Stephanie chatted with each other like nothing had happened, but neither had anything to say to Jordan and Justin, who sat just in front of them. There was stiff conversation between the two boys, even some laughter at one of Jordan's bad jokes, but it was clearly forced.

When it was time to break into math groups, things got even more awkward. Normally, the four friends would dive into a new problem with vigor, using teamwork to quickly come up with a solution. Today, without a word, they broke into separate teams. Jordan looked over at Catherine, who shrugged her shoulders in defeat. From that point on, it became clear that the two pairs were in direct competition to solve the latest problem from Mr. Miller.

A Knotty Problem

Use exactly four 4s to form every integer from 0 to 20, using only the following:

> **+, −, ×, ÷**
> **Parentheses**
> **Decimal point**
> **√ (Square root)**
> **! (Factorial)**
> **Example:** 0 = 4 + 4 − 4 − 4

"Okay, Justin, we've got this," Jordan said.

Justin gave an uneasy glance toward Stephanie and Catherine. They had their heads down and were already starting to work through the solution.

"Zero is already done, so only twenty numbers to go," Justin said. "Let's do this!"

Wait! Do you want to try this problem before the Math Kids do it?

Use only the four mathematical operations (+, −, ×, ÷), parentheses, decimal points, square roots (√), and factorials (!) and exactly four 4s to form every integer from 0 to 20.

If you need a refresher on the order of operations (what order to do calculations), you can refer to the appendix.

The first few were easy. Jordan and Justin quickly came up with solutions for 1 through 3.

$1 = 44 \div 44$
$2 = 4 \div 4 + 4 \div 4$
$3 = (4 + 4 + 4) \div 4$

The solution for 4 was a little trickier until Justin remembered that anything multiplied by 0 is just 0. That made the solution pretty easy.

$4 = 4 \times (4 - 4) + 4$

5 was also a snap.

$5 = (4 \times 4 + 4) \div 4$

"This is going to be easy," Jordan said.

Ten minutes later, Justin said, "I think you jinxed us." The solution for 6 had still not come to them. They could do it with three 4s ($4 + 4 \div \sqrt{4}$), but not with four of them. After several more minutes, they decided to go on to the next number.

"Got it!" Justin said. "44 divided by 4 gets us 11, then we just subtract the last 4."

$7 = 44 \div 4 - 4$

A Knotty Problem

"Nice!" Jordan said.

In the meantime, Stephanie and Catherine were also making fast work of the first ten numbers.

Stephanie made use of the square root operator to take care of 8.

$$8 = \sqrt{4} + \sqrt{4} + \sqrt{4} + \sqrt{4}$$

Catherine came up with a tricky way to solve for 9.

$$9 = 44 \div 4 - \sqrt{4}$$

"Nice work!" Stephanie exclaimed. "I had another way to do it, but I like yours better."

Both girls came up with a solution for 10 at the same time and they laughed as both wrote down the same answer.

$$10 = 4 + 4 + 4 - \sqrt{4}$$

"Halfway there," Catherine said. "How are you guys doing?"

Both Justin and Jordan looked up at her question.

"Same here," Justin said. "We've got all but a solution for the number 6."

"Really?" Stephanie asked. "That one was really easy." She looked down at the paper. "In fact, we've got four different solutions for that one."

"You do not!" Justin said, trying to look over at the girls' solution page.

"Trying to copy, Justin?" Catherine asked.

"No, I just don't believe you have four different ways for 6."

"Really?" Stephanie asked. "How about this one to start?" She showed him her equation:

$$4 + \sqrt{4} \times 4 \div 4$$

"That's only one," Justin shot back.

"Okay, how about $4 + (4 + 4) \div 4$?" Catherine asked. It was clear she was enjoying the fact the girls had multiple solutions for a problem the guys couldn't solve.

"And $(4 + 4 + 4) \div \sqrt{4}$," Stephanie said.

"And $\sqrt{4} + \sqrt{4} + 4 \div \sqrt{4}$," Catherine added.

"Now you're just showing off," Justin grumbled.

"It sounds like someone is a little jealous of our amazing math skills," Stephanie responded. Catherine giggled.

"We'll just see who gets to the end first," Jordan said determinedly.

He and Justin doubled their efforts and quickly found solutions for the next two numbers.

$$11 = 44 \div (\sqrt{4} + \sqrt{4})$$
$$12 = (44 + 4) \div 4$$

A Knotty Problem

They stumbled when they got to 13, so they decided to move on to 14, which Justin solved.

$$14 = 4 \times 4 - (4 \div \sqrt{4})$$

Justin's solution for 14 gave Jordan the inspiration for his answer for 15.

$$15 = 4 \times 4 - 4 \div 4$$

16 was a no brainer for the two, with both Justin and Jordan coming up with the easy answer.

$$16 = 4 + 4 + 4 + 4$$

Justin glanced over at the girls. It looked like they had also been stumped on a solution for 13 and had moved on to 17, putting them in a tie with him and Jordan.

"We've got to hurry, Jordan," he whispered. There was a note of desperation in his voice.

The girls had solved 17 and were now getting close to the end. Catherine had figured out that the answers for 15 and 17 were very similar.

$$17 = 4 \times 4 + 4 \div 4$$

Stephanie figured out 18.

$$18 = 4 \times 4 + 4 \div \sqrt{4}$$

Now they only had two to go and they could go back and tackle the tricky number 13. Except 19 also proved to be difficult. Neither Stephanie nor Catherine was able to quickly come up with a solution. Stephanie glanced at the boys' paper. They had skipped 19 and were working on 20.

Jordan nailed 20 and quickly scratched his answer onto the paper.

$$20 = 4 \times 4 + \sqrt{4} + \sqrt{4}$$

Catherine came up with a different answer.

$$20 = 4 \times (4 + 4 \div 4)$$

Both teams were now down to the same problems to solve: 13 and 19. It would be a race to the finish! Catherine was quickly trying various solutions. Jordan was scribbling on a piece of scratch paper, his pencil worn down to a small stub. Stephanie was examining previous answers to see if there was a similar method she could use for the last two problems. Justin was doing none of these things. He was just looking across the room.

Those who didn't know Justin would have thought he had become entranced with the bulletin board Mr. Miller had put up to illustrate the parts of speech. But when

A Knotty Problem

Jordan glanced over at his friend and saw him staring intently at the bulletin board, he smiled. He knew Justin was "in the zone," the place he went when he was trying to come up with a new idea. When Justin was in the zone, his mind was so focused that he lost track of everything else. One summer he had been thinking so hard about a quicker way to make his bed that he had walked right into the swimming pool. He had come up sputtering in the three-foot-deep water, but his plan of tying strings to the corners of the sheet and bedspread and pulling them to the head of the bed using a pulley system had worked rather well. Now Jordan was hoping he would come out of the zone with something that would allow them to finish the problem ahead of Stephanie and Catherine. He was not disappointed.

"Factorials!" Justin said, blinking his eyes to regain focus. "4 factorial is 24."

And that was all it took. Unfortunately, he had said it so loudly that now the girls knew as well. The race was on!

"Got 19!" yelled Catherine.

$$19 = 4! - 4 - 4 \div 4$$

"Me too!" said Justin just seconds later.

In the end, both teams approached the final answer in the same way. Knowing that 4 factorial was 24, they knew they had to find a way to subtract 11 to get to the final answer of 13. They scanned their previous solution for 11 and two hands scratched out a solution at the same time.

"Done!" Justin and Stephanie said in unison, scribbling their answers onto the paper.

$$13 = 4! - 44 \div 4$$

"We were first," Justin said.
"It was a tie," Stephanie replied.
"No way," Justin argued. "I definitely said it first."
"Well, I wrote it down first, so we won."
"Did not!"
"Did so!"
"What is going on over here?" came the gruff voice of Mr. Miller. "Is there some kind of problem?"
"We were racing to see who could answer the problem first and we won," Justin answered.
"Except you didn't," Stephanie said.
"I said it first," Justin said.
"I wrote it down first."
"No, you didn't," Justin countered.
"It was close," Jordan said, trying to calm them both. "Why don't we call it a tie?"
"It doesn't matter anyway," Stephanie said. "You guys needed help to get the number 6, so you wouldn't have even finished without us." She gave Justin a smug smile.

A Knotty Problem

"I'm with Jordan," Catherine said. "Let's call it a tie."

"But we won," Stephanie protested.

"I thought you four were a team," Mr. Miller said.

"Not anymore," Stephanie said. "Justin kicked Catherine and me out of the Math Kids."

"No, I didn't," Justin fumed. "You both quit."

"Only because you didn't give us a choice," Stephanie said. "You told us—"

"That's quite enough, you two," Mr. Miller interrupted. "Let's all return to our seats and we can discuss this later."

Chapter 4

The rest of the week didn't get any better. There was an icy silence whenever the four were together. At lunchtime, Stephanie and Catherine sat on one side of the cafeteria and the boys on the other. They avoided each other at recess and didn't say a word when they passed in the hallway. In their math group, the one time they were forced to be together, they worked in pairs instead of as a team. Jordan was happy to see the interminable week finally end. He was looking forward to the weekend. Jordan's sister Linda and his mom were going on a camping trip with some friends, so Jordan and his dad were going on a sailing trip.

Jordan's dad loved everything about ships. He was subscribed to four different magazines devoted to ships and sailing. He had built more than fifty ship models that he displayed in his home office. There was nothing he loved better than being out on the water. This weekend was going to be extra special because Jordan was going to get his first sailing lesson. His father had let him steer the fifty-six-foot sailboat a few times, but it was always in calm waters while using the ship's motor. This time it would be with full sails!

It was a two-hour drive to the coast. Jordan was quiet during the trip, staring out the window, unable to stop thinking about the situation with his friends. The harbor was a flurry of activity when they arrived. It seemed that everyone was taking advantage of the long weekend to get their boats out on the water. There were small two-person sailboats, pontoon boats carrying families, luxury ships with sleek lines and mahogany decks, and fishing boats with groups headed out in search of cod, haddock, and mackerel.

Jordan's dad co-owned the bright blue sailboat with Mr. Owens, a friend from work. Often, they went out together, taking Jordan and Mr. Owens's two sons, who were a few years older than Jordan. They already knew their way around the ship and how to handle the two sails, so Jordan just let them do the work while he enjoyed the view from the deck. This weekend it would just be him and his dad, so Jordan would have to help sail the ship. He knew that the mainsail was the large sail attached to the mast and the jib was the sail at the bow, or front, of the ship. He understood he needed to be very careful around the boom, the horizontal support for the mainsail. When the wind changed direction, the boom might

A Knotty Problem

swing from one side of the ship to the other, and it could give you quite a wallop if you were in the way. His dad had told him that's where the saying "lowering the boom" had come from.

"Okay, first lesson," his dad said when they reached the dock where their boat was moored.

"Ready to go, Dad," Jordan said as he hopped up onto the deck of the boat.

"The first lesson is actually down here," his dad said. He pointed to one of the ropes wrapped around a thick wooden column on the dock. "This is a clove hitch."

"Is that a kind of knot?"

"Yes, a hitch is a kind of knot we use when we want to put a rope around something, in this case this piling."

"Why don't we just have a loop of rope that could go over the top? Wouldn't that be easier?"

"It would, but not all docks have pilings like this. Some have rails that we need to tie around," his dad explained. "That's why one of the first things a sailor needs to know is how to tie some simple but important knots."

Jordan looked closely at the clove hitch. He was trying to figure out how he would tie it.

"A clove hitch isn't the most secure knot, but it does have some great advantages," his dad continued. "It is easy to tie and untie, and it can also be easily adjusted after it is tied."

"Can I try it?" Jordan asked.

"Sure," his dad answered. He untied the hitch and handed one end of the rope to Jordan. "It's a pretty easy knot to tie. Start by looping the rope around the piling."

Jordan looped one end of the rope around the thick wooden post.

"Okay, now you're going to loop it around again, only this time in the opposite direction. Then poke the end of the rope under your second loop."

Jordan followed his dad's instructions and looked at his handiwork.

"Like this?" Jordan asked.

"That's all there is to it. Now all we have to do is tighten it up a bit and we're good to go."

"That's cool," Jordan said, "but if it's not a very secure knot, aren't you worried it will come loose?"

A Knotty Problem

"We wouldn't rely on just one hitch," his dad explained. "If you look, you'll see that there are four different ropes tying the boat to the dock. They would all have to come loose at the same time and that's not likely to happen."

"That makes sense," Jordan said. As he looked at the four ropes, he noticed that two of them were different. "What about these two, Dad? They aren't tied to the poles."

"Pilings."

"Right, pilings. These other two are tied onto these metal things."

"That's right. Those are called cleats. And those knots are called cleat hitches. The cleat hitch is more secure than the clove hitch but is still easy to untie."

"Can I try that one too?" Jordan asked.

"That's why we're here," his dad answered. He quickly untied the knot and handed the rope to his son. "Now, this one is a little trickier than the clove hitch. See how the cleat has what looks like horns on both sides?"

Jordan nodded.

"Good, it will make it easier to explain if I can call them horns. Now, look at where we are pulling the line from the boat. One of the horns is closer and one is farther away, so I'll just call them the far horn and the near horn."

"Got it."

"Good. Okay, start by wrapping the rope around the far horn, around the near horn, and then over the top of the cleat."

It took a couple of tries, but Jordan managed to get through the first step.

"Great, now go under the far horn and then back over the top of the cleat."

Jordan looked confused, but with his dad walking him patiently through the next step, he was able to get it.

"Okay, only one more step. We want to make a loop with the rope and put it over the near horn."

Jordan got the loop backward the first time but got it right on his second attempt.

"Now let's tighten it up a bit and we're all done," his dad said. He pulled on the knot to make sure it was tight and then smiled. "Nice work, Jordan."

Jordan closely examined the cleat hitch he had just tied.

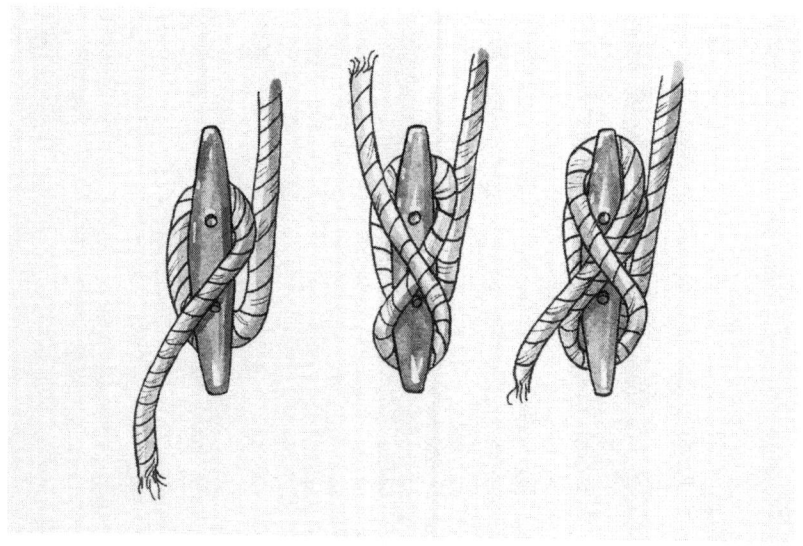

A Knotty Problem

"I'm not sure if I could do it again though."

"No big deal. I've got some rope in the garage at home so you can practice before our next trip. Now, what do you say we set sail?"

"Yeah!"

Jordan's dad got on the boat and started up the engine.

"Release the bow line," he called out. Jordan scurried to the front of the boat and released the clove hitch from the piling. He tossed the free end of the rope onto the deck of the boat. In a couple of minutes, he had untied all four lines securing the boat. He hopped onto the boat and his dad steered them into the channel between the docks. In a short time, they were out of the harbor and his dad cut the engine.

"Mind the boom, Jordan," he warned as he began to raise the main sail. A light breeze quickly filled the sail, and they were underway.

Normally Jordan just admired the scenery as they sailed. Today he paid close attention to everything his dad was doing, even taking a turn at adjusting the sails as the wind changed.

"I think I'm getting the hang of this," he said proudly as he remembered to duck when the boom swung across the deck.

The two sailed all afternoon, taking advantage of the winds to head south along the coast. They docked shortly before dinner. Jordan tied two perfect clove hitches to secure the boat. It took him three tries and some coaching from his dad to tie another cleat hitch, but he got the second one all on his own.

"A little sloppy but I think it will do the trick," he said as he examined the knot.

"Not too bad. Not too bad at all," his father said. "Now, how about some dinner?"

They feasted on fish and chips and had large slices of key lime pie for dessert, but Jordan still tried to talk his dad into ice cream as they walked back to the dock.

"Where do you put all that food?" his dad asked incredulously. "Do you have a hollow leg or something?"

"Hey, I did a lot of sailing today. I worked up a good appetite. So what do you think?"

"I think it's not going to happen. Your mom is already going to be mad if she hears about the pie."

"But I'm a growing boy," Jordan protested.

"Well, if you're still hungry when we get back to the boat, you can grab a couple handfuls of nuts. They'll keep you fuller than ice cream."

That night, as Jordan lay in his bunk on the boat, he thought about the new knots he had learned to tie. He wondered if there was something mathematical about knots. Maybe it was something he could ask Catherine's dad about the next time...and then he stopped. What if

A Knotty Problem

there wasn't a next time? What if the Math Kids were done for good?

That uneasy thought stuck in his mind, and it was a long time before the rocking of the boat and the crying of seagulls finally lulled him to sleep.

Chapter 5

"**H**ey, buddy, got a few minutes to talk?"

Justin looked up from the television show he was watching. His dad was standing in the doorway to the living room, a serious expression on his face. That meant it was probably not going to be a pleasant conversation.

"Sure, Dad." He paused the program, then changed his mind and turned off the television.

When he got to the kitchen, he saw his mom was already sitting at the table, spooning sugar into a cup of coffee. *Uh oh*, he thought. Now both parents wanted to talk to him, which was never a good sign.

"Is this about my room?" he asked. "Because I was planning on…"

"It's not about your room, sweetie," his mom answered. "Although now that you mention it—"

"One thing at a time," his dad cut in. His lips were set in a firm line and his brow was furrowed with what his mom called his "worry lines." Justin's mom looked down at the steam rising from her coffee cup.

A Knotty Problem

Now Justin was beginning to worry. What had he done? Overall, he thought he was a pretty good kid. He usually did what his parents asked. He followed the rules most of the time. His room was messy, but not nearly as bad as Jordan's. He got good grades, especially in math. He didn't talk back, at least not much. But the look on his dad's face was grim. What was going on?

"Do you remember the phone call I took last weekend? The work call?" his father asked.

"Kind of," Justin replied. "I think maybe it was your boss?"

"It wasn't from my boss. Well, not exactly. It was a call from another company. I've been offered a new job."

"Is it better than the one you have now?" Justin asked.

"Much better. I would be the vice president of research and development," his dad said.

"That's great, Dad!"

"It's a great opportunity for your father," his mom added. She glanced over at her husband.

Justin caught the look. "So what's the matter?"

"We would have to move," she said.

"Move? Move where? Would I still be in the same school?"

"No." There was a long pause as his father took a deep breath, afraid to break the news. "The job is in St. Louis."

"St. Louis? We would have to move to St. Louis?" Justin

asked. "But..." His words broke off as it dawned on him what this meant. "But what about Mom's job? She'd have to quit, too, wouldn't she?"

"You're right, and it will be hard for me too. You know how much I love working at the hospital," his mom said. Justin's mom was a nurse in the neonatal intensive care unit.

"See! Mom can't go!" Justin said.

"St. Louis has a number of large hospitals, so I'm sure I'll be able to find another nursing position," she replied. "I've thought a lot about it, and I'm on board with the move."

"It's a big decision for all three of us" his dad said. "But it's a great opportunity that I don't think I will ever get in my current company."

"What about other companies? Aren't there other jobs where we wouldn't have to move?"

"I've been looking for a while," his father said. "I don't think I'm going to get anything better than this. It's a software company that is putting out a new series of technical applications, and I would—"

"I don't care what they do," Justin interrupted. "What about my school, and the Math Kids? What about my friends? What about Jordan? How could you do this without even talking to me about it?" Hot tears streamed from his eyes. He angrily brushed them away, ran to his

A Knotty Problem

room, and slammed the door. Not satisfied, he opened it and slammed it again for good measure.

He flopped onto his bed and stared at the ceiling. How could his father do this to him? Now they would never be able to win the math competition. He thought about how much he wanted to answer that final question and watch the look of dejection on the faces of their opponents. He pictured himself holding up that trophy, his teammates raising their hands in triumph. The image of the trophy faded in his mind as he thought about his friends. Jordan, his best buddy for what seemed like forever. Catherine, the latest addition to the team, who always seemed to know some math the rest of the Math Kids didn't. And Stephanie...he didn't know what to think about her right now. She always seemed to put soccer over the Math Kids, but she always seemed to be there right when they needed her most. The four were a team, and maybe that meant more than a stupid trophy.

Justin finally came out of his room when his mom called him for supper. He didn't say much throughout the meal, just one-word answers to questions asked. Finally, his father had had enough.

"Look Justin, I know this news came as a shock, but we have to at least talk about it."

"What's there to talk about? You're making us move so you can have a better job."

"This is an opportunity for all of us," his dad responded.

"Is it?" Justin asked. "What exactly is my opportunity?"

"It's a chance to see a new part of the country, a bigger city than Maynard, for one," his dad said. "I think you'll like St. Louis. They have a great zoo, a science center, professional sports teams, an aquarium, and a really cool children's museum."

"And let's not forget the Gateway Arch," his mother added. "It's six hundred and thirty feet tall, and you can ride all the way to the top to look out."

"Sounds like a great place for a *visit*," Justin responded sarcastically. "Maybe we should go there sometime."

"You're not giving this much of a chance, Justin," his mother said.

"I'm giving it about as much chance as you gave me."

"That's not fair," his father said, a tinge of anger in his voice.

"Fair? You're moving me away from all of my friends and you think I'm the one not being fair?"

Justin's father had no response. He picked up his dinner dishes and took them to the sink. Then he walked out the sliding glass door and sank into a chair on the back deck. He stared at the sun setting through the trees. Inside, Justin watched his father in silence.

"You know this is a really difficult decision for your dad, don't you?" his mother asked.

"Yeah, I know, but..."

A Knotty Problem

"And you know he only wants what's best for our family, right?"

"Yeah, but..."

"And there's one other thing you should know."

"What's that?" Justin asked.

"Even though he is really excited about the opportunity, he hasn't accepted the job yet."

"He hasn't? Why not?"

"I think you know the answer to that," Justin's mom said quietly.

Justin thought before answering. "Because he wants it to be okay with me?"

"That's right."

"Then we really don't have to move?" Justin asked.

"If you think that's the best thing for the family, I guess you're right."

Justin thought about this while he watched his dad staring into the distance.

"He's worked really hard for this, hasn't he?" he finally asked.

"He has."

"If he took the job, when would we have to move?"

"We would stay here until the end of the school year."

"Why?" Justin asked.

"Your dad didn't want you to miss the district math competition."

Tears welled in Justin's eyes.

David Cole

He turned away from his mom as he quickly blinked the tears away. After a moment to compose himself, he slid the glass door open and stepped out onto the deck.

"So tell me more about this really cool children's museum."

Chapter 6

"I have a great idea," Mr. Duchesne said at breakfast. Catherine looked up from her pancakes. "You always have great ideas."

"Of course, but this one is extra great," he said. "It solves one of the biggest issues in the world today."

"I'm guessing it has something to do with math," she said.

"Of course," he said. "Are there great ideas that don't have something to do with math?"

Catherine laughed. "I could probably come up with some, but I'm sure you'd somehow find a way to relate them to math."

"Exactly. So here's my idea—word problems."

Catherine raised her eyebrows. She smiled, not quite sure if her dad was being serious. "Word problems?"

"Word problems."

"Are you saying that word problems are the biggest issue in the world today?" Catherine asked.

"Well, maybe not quite on the scale of global warming,

pandemics, and stuff like that, but still pretty important, at least to mathematicians," her dad responded.

"Why?"

"You see, there are very few pure mathematicians in the world," her dad said.

"What's a pure mathematician?"

"Great question. Pure mathematics is the study of the underlying concepts and structures of mathematics. A pure mathematician is always searching for a deeper understanding of these concepts. An applied mathematician, on the other hand, applies these mathematical concepts to solve problems, whether it is science, engineering, or some other area."

"Which one are you, pure or applied?"

Her father laughed. "I guess you would say I'm a little of both. I love to figure out new math concepts, but I also love to solve problems."

"And what do word problems have to do with this conversation and solving the world's problems?"

"Well, you know me—I think math can solve most problems. The issue has always been in translating the actual problem to the math that can solve it. That's where word problems come in."

"I'm not sure if I understand," Catherine said. She poured more syrup on her pancakes and took a large bite while she waited for her father's explanation.

A Knotty Problem

"The problem with word problems is that it's sometimes hard to get to the actual problem."

"There are a lot of *problems* in that sentence," Catherine said.

"True. Let me rephrase. If there was an easier way to translate the words into equations, I think people would have better luck in solving them." He thought for a moment. "Let me give you an example. Bill is four times as old as Wanda. Twelve years ago, Bill was seven times as old as Wanda. How old is Wanda now?"

Catherine immediately pushed her breakfast aside and reached for a pencil and a piece of paper.

> Wait! Do you want to try to solve this problem before Catherine does?
>
> Bill is four times as old as Wanda. Twelve years ago, Bill was seven times as old as Wanda. How old is Wanda now?

"That's an easy one, Dad," Catherine said.

"I thought you'd say that. Show me how you would solve it."

"I start with the first equation. Bill is four times as old as Wanda. I'll use the letter B for Bill and the letter W for Wanda to make it easier."

She wrote the first equation at the top of the page.

$$B = 4W$$

"The second equation is similar. Twelve years ago, Bill was seven times as old as Wanda," she said. She added the second equation to the page.

$$B - 12 = 7W$$

"Are you sure about that equation?" her dad asked.
"I think so," Catherine said.
"Why is it B − 12?"
"Because that's how old Bill was twelve years ago. B is his age today and B − 12 is his age twelve years ago."
"And how old was Wanda twelve years ago?" he asked.
"Ouch, that's right! I need to subtract twelve years from her age too," Catherine said. She scratched out the equation and wrote the new one beneath it.

$$B - 12 = 7(W - 12)$$

"Much better," her dad said. "So now you have two equations. What's next?"
"Well, I need to get rid of one of the variables, either the B or the W, in one of the equations. Since I know that B equals 4W from the first equation, I'll just substitute 4W for the B in the second equation." She wrote the new equation.

A Knotty Problem

$$4W - 12 = 7(W - 12)$$

"And now I'll multiply everything out to simplify it," she said. She wrote this on the paper.

$$4W - 12 = 7W - 84$$

"Looking good," her father said encouragingly.

"Now I'll subtract 4W from both sides." She wrote the new equation.

$$-12 = 3W - 84$$

"And add 84 to both sides."

$$72 = 3W$$

"Finally, I'll divide each side by 3 and I should have the answer."

$$W = 24$$

"That means Wanda is twenty-four years old now," she said triumphantly.

"Did you check your answer?" her dad asked.

"Doing that now," Catherine answered. "If Wanda is twenty-four today and Bill is four times as old, that would make him ninety-six years old. Twelve years ago, he would have been eighty-four and Wanda would have been twelve. Twelve times seven is eighty-four, so it all checks out."

"Well done," her dad praised her work. "Well thought out and executed. The problem is that lots of people couldn't have figured out how to come up with the two equations you started out with."

"And I got one of them wrong," Catherine said.

"Right. You're one of the smartest kids I know and even you made a small mistake that would have made it impossible to solve the problem. Still, most people wouldn't have the first idea how to even start. They just can't translate the words into math. That translation is what I'm trying to solve."

"Wow! You know, kids all over the world would thank you if you could help them solve word problems," Catherine exclaimed.

"Not just kids," her dad corrected. "Think for a moment about big complex issues like climate change. One of the problems is trying to figure out how to express the problem in terms that allow people to work on solving it. We have lots of numbers, like rate of change of ocean temperature, carbon dioxide emissions by country, percent of renewable energy usage, and so on, but we need to find the best way to put these numbers together

A Knotty Problem

into equations that will help us to figure out the best approach to solving the problem."

"And that's where your idea comes in?"

"Exactly. I want to develop an application that will take words and numbers and translate them into solvable math equations. I'd start with easy word problems to prove out the concept. We'd then be able to build a knowledge base that would allow us to solve more and more complex problems."

"That's amazing, Dad," Catherine said. "But do you think you can really do it?"

"Maybe not, but I'm sure going to give it a try," he said. "The problem is resources. I've got a full schedule teaching at the university and only have so much time I can devote to this project. Maybe if I was able to get some funding, I might be able to hire some software developers and mathematicians to get it off the ground."

"You'll figure it out, Dad. You always do," Catherine said.

"I hope so." He rubbed a finger over his lower lip as he thought for a moment. "Speaking of problems, are you and your friends any closer to a reconciliation of the Math Kids?"

"Not yet. It was a miserable week, but hopefully we'll get something figured out soon."

Chapter 7

For Justin, the next week was a blur. On Monday morning, his dad flew out to St. Louis to meet with the management team at the new company. He still hadn't officially accepted the job, but it was mostly just working out the details of the employment contract before it became a done deal. On Wednesday, his dad spent the day with a real estate agent to start the search for a new house. Justin heard his mom talking with him on the phone that evening. He heard snippets of the conversation, mostly questions from his mom about school districts, number of bedrooms and bathrooms, and sizes of backyards. While his mom sounded enthusiastic, for Justin the conversation was depressing. It was like they had crossed a threshold from which there was no return. It certainly didn't help that tensions were still high at school, just another problem on his growing list.

He was still trying to accept the fact he would be moving from his hometown and the only house he had ever known. He loved his room with its two window

A Knotty Problem

alcoves with cushioned seating—perfect for reading or just looking out the window into the backyard. His walk-in closet was packed with his "valuables": a thick cardboard tube he was planning to use to build his own telescope; a plastic container filled with spools of wire, batteries, switches, gears, wheels, and other components for the robot he hoped to create one day; at least three decks of mismatched playing cards he could use to learn magic tricks to amaze his friends; and stacks of boxes with various odds and ends that might somehow fit into one of his project ideas.

A poster of Albert Einstein was taped on the wall over his bed, the scientist's white hair a disheveled mess as if he had more important things to do than to comb it. Under his picture was Justin's favorite quote from the famous physicist: "If you can't explain it simply, you don't understand it well enough." It made him think about Mr. Miller, his fifth-grade teacher, who had struggled to teach math because he didn't understand it well enough.

On another wall, there was a poster of mathematician Leonard Euler saying, "Mathematicians have tried in vain to this day to discover some order in the sequence of prime numbers, and we have reason to believe that it is a mystery into which the human mind will never penetrate." To Justin, that quote was a reminder that there was still more to conquer in the field of mathematics. He had bought the poster after he, Stephanie, and Jordan had been able to thwart the burglars who had been using the randomness of prime numbers to pick their next target. Now it was a sad reminder of the friendships he would be losing when he moved to St. Louis.

He still hadn't been able to tell Jordan, who had been his best friend since kindergarten. They had been through so much over the years that he was struggling to find a good time to break the news to him. And what about Catherine and Stephanie? Even though things were a little rocky right now, they were still his friends, weren't they?

It was amazing how quickly things had turned around. Only two weeks ago, Justin and his friends had been

A Knotty Problem

strategizing about how to win the district math competition. Now the team was cut in half and was about to be dealt yet another blow with Justin's news.

Justin's thoughts were interrupted by his mom entering his bedroom. He looked up as she placed a stack of socks and underwear on his bed.

"Can you put these away for me?" she asked.

"Sure," he said absently.

"I was thinking maybe we'd have the Waters over for a barbecue this weekend. What do you think?"

"I don't know," he answered. "I still haven't told Jordan the news yet."

"Would it be easier if we told them at the barbeque?"

"Maybe. I don't know. I should probably let him know myself, just the two of us, you know?"

"Kind of man to man, you mean?" his mom asked.

"Yeah, I guess. It's just that it's going to be so hard to find a way to tell him. Do I break it to him gently or just get it over with quickly?"

"That question reminds me of a joke I heard a long time ago," his mom said. "A guy was on vacation and asked his brother to take care of his cat while he was gone. A week later he called to check in. 'How's the cat?' he asked. 'He's dead,' the brother replied. 'What?' the first man said. 'You can't just blurt out bad news like that. You have to break it to me gently.' His brother asked how he would do that. 'Well,' the man said, 'you could say that the cat was on the roof and wouldn't come down. Then maybe you could say it fell off. You took it to the vet, who tried everything, but unfortunately the cat passed away.' 'Oh, I get it now,' said the brother. 'I'm glad,' said the man. 'By the way, how is Mom doing?' The brother took a long breath and said, 'She's on the roof and won't come down.'"

Justin laughed, something he hadn't done since he had first heard the news about moving. "That's a good one, Mom," he said. "So you're suggesting that I break it to him gently?"

"It's up to you, Justin, but I'll tell you this. The band aid is going to come off whether you pull it gently or rip it off. Me, I prefer to get that thing off as quickly as possible."

Justin thought about that for a minute. "Maybe I'll try something in between."

His mom raised an eyebrow. "What are you thinking?"

"I think I'm going to tell him Dad pushed the cat off the roof."

His mom laughed. "So you'll talk to Jordan before the barbeque?"

"I will, but there's someone else I need to talk to first."

***

He was the last person Stephanie expected to see, so her jaw dropped when Justin showed up at her practice. He

A Knotty Problem

had his hands tucked deeply into the pockets of his hoodie, and he looked miserable. When practice finished, her first thought was to just ignore him and go home, but something about the look on Justin's face stopped her, so she walked slowly toward him.

"What do you want? You need more help with a math problem?" she asked sarcastically.

"Um, this doesn't have anything to do with math," Justin said.

"Good, because you kicked me out of the Math Kids, remember?"

The comment stung, but Justin held back his anger. "Yeah, I remember. I really just came to ask you a question."

"So go ahead and ask," she said.

"What was it like for you when you moved here?"

Stephanie raised her eyebrows. It was not a question she was expecting. "Well," she said thoughtfully, "I guess it was kind of hard at first. When my mom said we were moving, I couldn't believe it. Especially right in the middle of a school year."

Stephanie's statement made Justin really appreciate his dad's decision to at least wait to move until after the school year was over.

"Was it hard to make new friends?" Justin asked.

"A little, but I joined the soccer team and that helped me meet a lot of new girls. And then...well, then I met people at school too."

Justin thought back to that day when Stephanie had marched into their fourth-grade classroom and announced herself to the world. She had made it look so easy. Justin didn't think he would ever have the nerve to do something like that.

"Yeah, I kind of remember that," Justin said. The memory brought a half-smile to his face. "It seems like a long time ago, doesn't it?"

"I guess," Stephanie said. "So why the questions about me moving here?"

Justin took a deep breath. "Well, my dad has this new job, and we'll be moving at the end of the school year."

Stephanie gasped. "You're moving? Where to?"

"St. Louis."

"I'm really sorry to hear that, Justin," Stephanie said sincerely.

"Yeah, me too," Justin said. "Anyway, I just wanted you to know and see if maybe you had any advice for me."

"I don't know if I have any advice," Stephanie said. "But I know this, Justin. You'll be okay. You might not believe that now, but you will be okay."

Justin thought about this before responding. "Thanks, Stephanie. I really appreciate it. And about the Math Kids…"

"I don't want to talk about that, Justin," Stephanie said. "You may not get it, but you really hurt Catherine and me when you threw us out." She turned and walked quickly away, leaving Justin alone on the field.

Chapter 8

The barbecue was scheduled for Sunday afternoon, so by Sunday morning Justin had run out of time. It was now or never. He walked across the street to Jordan's house and knocked softly on the door. Jordan answered, wearing a ridiculous pair of orange-and-white-checkered checkered shorts paired with a red-and-green-striped shirt. It was the kind of mismatched outfit that normally would have brought a hilarious response from Justin, but not today.

"Hey, Justin."

"Hi, Jordan. Can I come in for a few minutes?"

"Sure, what's up?"

"It's kind of private. Can we go to your room?" Justin asked.

"Okay," Jordan said hesitantly. "Is something going on?"

"Yeah, I guess you could say that," Justin said, but then remained silent until they were alone in Jordan's room with the door closed.

"Is there a problem at home?" Jordan asked anxiously.

"No. It's just that…"

"You're killing me, man. Whatever it is, just come out and say it already."

Justin took a deep breath and yanked the band aid. "My dad got a new job with a company in St. Louis. We're moving there as soon as the school year is over."

There wasn't a sound for what seemed an interminable time. It felt like Justin's words had sucked all the air out of the room, leaving its inhabitants unable to take a breath. Justin held his friend's gaze at first, but then had to look away as he saw the tears start to flow. Now his own began to well up and drip slowly down his cheeks. And still there wasn't a sound.

***

The barbecue got off to a horrible start. Justin's dad overcooked the burgers and his mom had forgotten to buy buns.

"Looks like we're stuck with sandwich bread," Justin's mom said quietly to her husband so the guests seated around the table on the deck wouldn't hear.

"They'll go great with these burnt burgers," he responded. "Well, at least we have plenty of fixings for the burgers. Maybe no one will notice."

A Knotty Problem

The fixings didn't help. Even Justin, who would eat pretty much anything, didn't have much of an appetite. Just as they began to eat, the skies opened, and everyone had to rush into the house to get out of the sudden downpour.

"Oh my," Justin's mom said by way of apology, "could this day get any worse?"

"You can't control the weather," Jordan's mom consoled.

"Maybe not, but I can control the shopping list. I'm so sorry I forgot the buns."

"I don't know that buns would have helped these burgers," Justin's dad said. He held up a burger and looked at it closely.

"What are you doing, dear?"

"Just trying to make sure this is a burger and not one of the charcoal briquettes."

"At least we have dessert," Justin's mom said brightly.

"Do we?" Justin asked. He pointed out the sliding back door. The chocolate layer cake sat on the table in the pouring rain. It was soaked, rivulets of chocolate icing running down its sides and onto the table.

His mom looked sadly at the cake and shook her head.

"Okay, who's up for pizza?" she asked loudly.

Things got better after that. Justin's dad ordered pizza. His mom found some ready-to-bake cookies in the refrigerator and baked two dozen while they waited.

The pizzas were delivered forty-five minutes later, one pepperoni, one veggie, and one meat lovers, Justin's favorite. It was covered with bacon, sausage, pepperoni, and ham.

The inevitable conversation came up while they munched on slices of pizza and nibbled on chocolate chip cookies.

"I don't know if Jordan told you, but Tom was offered a position at a company in St. Louis," Justin's mom said. "It's a really nice promotion."

Jordan's parents nodded. "We'll hate to see you leave," Jordan's mom said, "but it sounds like one of those opportunities you just can't turn down."

"It is," Justin's dad said. "High tech software, a new product line, a big bump in my responsibilities. It's something I've just not been able to find in Maynard."

"I guess I'm going to have to find a new golf partner," Jordan's dad said.

"Maybe you can find someone who can keep the ball out of the water," Justin's dad said.

"Seriously, though, we'll miss you guys. You've been great neighbors and even better friends."

"That's very nice of you to say," Justin's mom said. She looked away as she felt tears coming.

Justin took the opportunity to catch Jordan's eye. He nodded his head toward the living room. Jordan nodded.

"We're going to go play some video games," Justin

A Knotty Problem

announced. Without waiting for a response, the boys got up from the table and headed toward the living room. Twenty seconds later, Justin was back. He grabbed the plate with the remaining cookies.

"Need a little energy food," he said. "It's not easy defending Earth from aliens, you know."

In the next room, Jordan and Justin absentmindedly shot lasers at unwanted visitors from the planet Neutron while they talked.

"This really stinks," Jordan said.

"I know."

"And there's no way to change your dad's mind?"

"I doubt it," Justin replied as he tossed a grenade over a wall, obliterating a squad of alien scouts. "He said it's the perfect job for him. He's going to be the head of software development on a whole new product line."

"Yeah, sounds too good to pass up. Unless..."

"Unless what?" Justin asked.

"Well, what if he could find something like that here in Maynard?"

"That's just it. He's been looking for more than a year. There's nothing out there."

"But if there was, would he change his mind?" Jordan asked.

"I guess it's a possibility."

"Then that's the problem we have to solve."

"It's not a problem we can solve," Justin protested.

"All problems can be solved," Jordan said.

"This isn't math, Jordan," Justin said, tossing his controller down on the couch. "It's real life. It's *my* life. And I guess I'm going to get used to the fact that my life is now going to be in St. Louis."

"Yeah, I guess you're right," Jordan said. He looked at his friend and saw how unhappy he was.

"But at least we can make the most out of the time we have left," Justin said.

"What do you mean?"

"Well, maybe the Math Kids can't win the district math competition, but the four of us can still solve a bunch of fun math problems before I go," Justin said.

"But Stephanie and Catherine are still mad at us."

"Yeah, but maybe I can do something about that," Justin said.

Chapter 9

At lunch on Monday, Justin took a deep breath and walked over to the table where Stephanie and Catherine were eating. Jordan followed in his wake.

"Hey. Jordan and I have been talking," Justin began.

Stephanie didn't reply.

Justin took a breath and continued. "We were thinking that maybe we could call a truce."

"A truce?" Catherine asked.

"Yeah, a truce," Justin answered. "Like even if we can't go to the district championship because of the stupid soccer—"

Jordan coughed and elbowed his friend in the side.

Justin started again. "I mean, at least we could still work together on math problems in class."

"Why would we want to do that?" Catherine asked.

"Well, it's just that it's more fun when the four of us work together," Justin said.

"We're a pretty good team, remember?" Jordan added.

"Is this because you're moving?" Stephanie asked.

Jordan looked up in surprise. "Wait! How did you know Justin was moving? I only found out yesterday."

A Knotty Problem

"He told me when he came to my soccer practice on Thursday."

"You told Stephanie before you told me?" Jordan asked.

"You've lived here all your life. She knows more about this moving stuff than you do. It had to have been hard for her to move here last year, so I figured she could give me some advice."

"I still can't believe you helped him after the way he treated us," Catherine said.

"Yeah, surprised me a little bit too," Stephanie admitted.

"Well, at least you're going to be here until the end of the school year, Justin," Catherine said.

"Wait, you knew about him moving too?" Jordan asked. "Was I seriously the last to know?"

"You really didn't think Stephanie would keep that information to herself, did you?" Catherine asked.

Jordan looked at Justin, who shrugged his shoulders.

Stephanie looked over at Catherine and raised an eyebrow. "So what do you think about a truce?"

Catherine looked at Justin and then back at Stephanie. "I guess I'm okay with that if you are."

"But it's just a truce," Stephanie said. "Now, if you don't mind, we'd like to get back to our lunch."

"I get it," Justin replied. "I guess we'll see you in math then."

The two boys walked away, Justin shuffling along as he stared down at his feet.

When the boys had left, Catherine turned back to Stephanie. "Are you really okay with this truce?"

"The truce is just for math," Stephanie said. "As far as I'm concerned, nothing else has changed."

"Sounds like you're still pretty mad at Justin."

"Yeah, but I would like to do math as a team again."

"I do miss that," Catherine said.

"It's still too bad that we won't be able to be in the math competition."

"I'm not so sure about that," Catherine said.

"What do you mean?" Stephanie asked. "I still have my soccer tournament."

"I've been thinking about that," Catherine said.

In fact, Catherine had been thinking about the scheduling conflict since she first spoke about it with her dad. If the math competition and soccer tournament had not been scheduled for the same weekend, Justin never would have gotten upset and she and Stephanie never would have quit the Math Kids. If they could fix the scheduling conflict, maybe it would fix everything.

"What if we were able to get the math competition moved to another weekend?"

"How can we do that?"

"Think back to last year's competition," Catherine said.

"I try not to," Stephanie said. "The Mathketeers from Armstrong stomped us in the final round."

"But think about what happened after. Do you remember what their captain said?"

A Knotty Problem

When Stephanie didn't answer, she went on. "He said if it wasn't for the Math Kids, there wouldn't even be a competition."

"I remember that now," Stephanie said. "But what does that have to do with this year's competition?"

"Well, I think they owe us one," Catherine said. "So I'm going to ask the school board to move the date for us."

"Do you think they'll do it?"

"We won't know unless we ask. The next board meeting is on Thursday night. You want to go with me?"

"I'm in!"

"Then here's what I'm thinking," Catherine said. She told Stephanie about her plans for the meeting.

When Mr. Miller said it was time for math that afternoon, the Math Kids assembled in their usual spot in the back corner of the classroom.

Mr. Miller approached the group with a sheet of paper. "Okay, I think I found a tricky problem for you today," he said. He placed the paper on the desk.

They looked at the problem.

> *An old man died, leaving his three daughters and their husbands a total of $1,000 in his will. Altogether the daughters received $396. Annabelle received $10 more than Becky and Carla received $10 more than Annabelle. Frank Smith received the same amount as his wife. Ethan Corbin received one and*

a half times as much as his wife. Dave Sanders received twice as much as his wife. What is the married name of each daughter?

> Wait! Do you want to try to solve this problem before the Math Kids do? Using the clues, can you figure out which daughter is married to which husband?

"This looks easy enough," Jordan said.

"I hate it when you say that," Justin replied.

"Why?"

"Because it always ends up being more difficult than you thought."

Justin turned out to be correct.

"Okay, let's start by writing down what we know," Stephanie said. She opened her notebook and retrieved a pencil and a sheet of paper. "Let's start with the wives. Let's call them *A*, *B*, and *C*. We know they got $396." She wrote the first equation on her paper.

$$A + B + C = 396$$

"We also know that Annabelle received ten dollars more than Becky and Carla received ten dollars more than Annabelle," Catherine said. She wrote down the two equations.

A Knotty Problem

$A = B + 10$
$C = A + 10$

"That should be enough to figure out how much each daughter got," Jordan said. "First, we can rearrange the formula for A a little." He scratched $B = A - 10$ on the page. "So we can just get rid of the B and C variables using the two new equations," he continued.

Substituting for B and C, Stephanie wrote

$A + B + C = 396$
$A + (A - 10) + (A + 10) = 396$

Since the 10s just canceled each other out, they were left with a new equation with only A as a variable,

$3A = 396$
which meant
$A = 132$

"Great work!" Catherine said. "So Annabelle got $132. Since that was $10 more than Becky, Becky got $122. And since Carla received $10 more than Annabelle, she got $142."

Stephanie recorded this new information on the paper.

Annabelle $132   Becky $122   Carla $142

"Okay, we know what the daughters got. We also know that the husbands must have received $604 since the total is $1,000," Justin said.

"I told you this would be easy," Jordan said. "We're on a roll."

And then they weren't. That's where the problem got tricky. Since they didn't know which daughter was married to which husband, they weren't sure how to figure out the next step. They only knew that Frank Smith got the same amount as his wife, Ethan Corbin received one and a half times as much as his wife, and Dave Sanders got twice as much as his wife.

After staring at the problem for ten minutes with no progress, it was finally Catherine who got them going again.

"Here's an idea," she said. "What if we listed each of the possibilities for each wife. For example, we know that Annabelle received $132. If she was married to Frank, he would have also received $132, right? If she was married to Ethan, he would have received one and a half times as much, or $198. And if she was married to Dave, he would have gotten twice as much, or $264."

"I get where you're going with this, Catherine," Justin said. "We should then be able to pick the right combination that would add up to $604."

Catherine wrote the combinations on the paper, and everyone began calculating in their heads.

A Knotty Problem

	Received	Frank	Ethan	Dave
Annabelle	132	132	198	264
Becky	122	122	183	244
Carla	142	142	213	284

"Wait, I think I found something," Stephanie blurted out.

Everyone looked at her in anticipation.

"What have you got, Stephanie?" asked Jordan.

Stephanie pointed at the numbers in the Ethan column. "All of the numbers are even except for these two. If Becky or Carla are married to Ethan, we get an odd number."

"So?" Justin asked.

"So when we add the total for all of the husbands together, we have to come up with 604, which is even," she explained. "We can't add two even numbers and one odd number and come up with an even number."

"That would mean that Annabelle must be the one married to Ethan!" Catherine said.

"Nice!" Jordan said. "Okay, if she is married to Ethan, he got $198. That means the other two husbands received a total of $406. We just need to find the combination that adds up to $406."

"Got it!" Justin said. "It must be Carla married to Dave, who got $284, and Becky married to Frank, who got $122. That adds up to $406!"

"Perfect," Stephanie said. "That means the daughters'

full names are Annabelle Corbin, Becky Smith, and Carla Sanders."

Justin looked around at his teammates. It was almost like nothing had ever happened.

"That was great teamwork," Justin said. "Hey, speaking of that, did you see the new TV show about—"

"The truce was about math," Stephanie interrupted. "Solving the problem was fun, but math time is over now."

Chapter 10

The school board meeting was on Thursday evening.

Stephanie was wearing a blue dress with leggings underneath. Catherine had on a nice pair of black pants with a blouse and light green sweater.

Stephanie smiled. "We clean up pretty nicely, don't we?"

Catherine smiled back but looked nervous about walking into the meeting.

"You'll be fine," Stephanie assured her.

They walked in together and sat in the back in a row of folding chairs. They waited patiently as the board members went through the minutes from the previous meeting and discussed old business. They debated and then voted on a proposal for new books for ninth grade biology class.

New business came next. It was mostly about the budget, which, unlike the previous year, looked very solid. There was even a discussion about adding a new performing arts auditorium that would be shared between the middle and high schools.

"That's all thanks to us finding that gold," Stephanie said quietly.

Finally, it was time for open discussion from the audience. Several parents asked about making changes to the high school dress code. The high school football coach wanted new grass for the practice field. When the line to the microphone grew short, Catherine looked at Stephanie and nodded. It was time. The two joined the line.

Catherine coughed as she approached the microphone, trying hard to disguise her nervousness.

"Yes, young lady?" Mr. Bilson, the president of the school board prompted.

"Um, yes. I'd like to ask about—"

"Can you please state your name for the record?" a red-haired lady asked from the end of the long table at the front of the room.

"Um, sure. I'm Catherine Duchesne. I'm in fifth grade at—"

"And will your friend also be speaking?" the lady asked.

"Yes, ma'am. Like I said, I'm in—"

"And can I get her name too?" the woman interrupted for the third time.

A Knotty Problem

Catherine looked at her in frustration, and Stephanie leaned toward the microphone to answer.

"My name is Stephanie Lewis."

"Thank you," the woman said. "Please continue."

"Thank you," Catherine said. "I am in the fifth grade at McNair Elementary. My friends and I competed in the district math competition last year."

"Congratulations," Mr. Bilson said.

"For what?" Catherine asked.

"For participating in the math competition," he responded.

"But we didn't win."

"It's not always about winning. It's about doing your best."

"Yeah, I guess, but we sure wanted to win," Catherine said.

"Of course," the school board president said with a smile.

"Anyway, we're planning on being in the competition again this year."

"Good for you," Mr. Bilson said.

"But we can't," Catherine said.

Mr. Bilson looked at Catherine over the top of his thick glasses. "Is there someone who says you can't participate?"

"No," Catherine said. "But we do have a conflict with the date."

"The date?"

"Yes, sir," Stephanie chimed in. "You see, the math competition is the same weekend as the girls state soccer tournament I'm in."

"Oh, that's too bad," Mr. Bilson said. "I guess you'll have to choose one."

"No, sir," Catherine said firmly. "She wants to choose both."

"But I don't see how that's possible," Mr. Bilson said.

Catherine looked down at her notes and found what she was looking for. "Andrew Wiles said, 'Just because we can't find a solution, it doesn't mean there isn't one.'"

Several board members looked at each other. One asked, "And who is Andrew Wiles?"

"He's an English mathematician," Catherine answered. "He's the one who proved Fermat's Last Theorem."

Mrs. Guidry, the school board vice president smiled. "Well, I have to admit I was never very good at math myself." Several other board members laughed.

"I hope you don't take offense, ma'am," Stephanie said, "but we don't think math is a laughing matter."

Mrs. Guidry stopped smiling and stared intently at Stephanie. "Miss Lewis, is it?" she asked.

"Yes, ma'am."

"What exactly is it you are asking this board to do?"

"I'd like to be able to participate in both my soccer tournament and the math competition," she said.

A Knotty Problem

"I don't see how you can do that. You can't be in two places at the same time, you know," Mrs. Guidry said smugly.

"That's correct, Mrs. Guidry," Catherine said. "But, as George Polya once said, 'If you can't solve a problem, then there is an easier problem you can solve: find it.'"

"And who is George Polya? Another mathematician, I assume?"

"That's right, ma'am," Catherine answered. "He's a Hungarian mathematician known as the father of modern problem-solving."

"And he has a solution for the problem of being in two places at the same time?" Mrs. Guidry asked.

"No, but we can solve an easier problem. You see, a person can't be in two places at the same time, but a person can certainly be in two places at two different times," Catherine said. "We're asking if the math competition can be moved to another weekend."

"I'm afraid that's out of the question," Mrs. Guidry said. "Dates are set well in advance so people can work out their schedules accordingly. Now, I'm sorry that you won't be able to participate, Miss Lewis, but it's not fair to the other kids if we move the date just to accommodate you."

"But—" Catherine started before being interrupted by Mrs. Guidry.

"I'm sorry, but I think we've spent enough time on this

topic. The district math competition will remain at its original date."

"Then I'm afraid we won't be able to attend," came a voice from the crowd.

"Who is that?" asked the red-haired secretary. She peered over her glasses at the crowd.

A tall blond boy rose from his seat. "I'm Josh Benson. I'm from Armstrong Elementary, and our team won the district math championship last year. If the Math Kids from McNair can't participate, then neither can we."

Another student rose. "I'm here to represent Wright Elementary. We also won't be able to participate."

"Us either," said a short girl from the second row. She could barely see over the seated man in front of her. "I'm Isabella Manuel from Maynard Elementary."

Students from Twillman and Eastman elementary schools also chimed in, saying they wouldn't be participating without McNair either.

In front of the microphone, Catherine tried hard not to smile. She was glad she had thought to reach out to the other teams. It was just the wildcard they needed right now.

"I see," said Mrs. Guidry. "Well, I guess it wouldn't be much of a competition without any teams, would it?" She consulted a calendar and spoke quietly with the president. "Would the following weekend work for all of the teams?"

"That certainly works for us," Catherine said. "How about everyone else?"

A Knotty Problem

All the students who had spoken up smiled and nodded their assent.

"We'll send out an announcement to all of the schools then," Mrs. Guidry said. "Well played, Miss Duchesne." She gave her a short nod of respect.

When the meeting ended, Catherine made it a point to thank each of the students from the other schools who had spoken on their behalf.

"No worries, happy to help," said Josh Benson. "But just so you know, we won't be holding anything back at the competition. We plan to repeat as champions."

"And we plan to make sure that doesn't happen," Catherine said solemnly.

"Game on then," Josh said.

The next day at school, Catherine broke the news to Jordan and Justin that the math competition was back on.

"What? How did you do that?" Jordan asked.

"Oh, I pulled a few strings," Catherine replied. She explained how the other teams had come to the meeting to support her.

"That's cool, Catherine. Nice job!" Jordan exclaimed.

"It will be nice to have the team back together for one more shot," Justin said. He looked over at Stephanie for confirmation.

She nodded but held up a finger. "It's just for the math, Justin. Remember that."

Chapter 11

On Saturday, the Math Kids planned an all-day session of problem-solving at Catherine's house. There were some periods of tenseness between Justin and Stephanie, but they still worked together well as a team. When one person struggled, someone else always stepped up to offer another approach that got them going again. After a couple of hours of working through problems, Mr. Duchesne entered with a plate of mini-muffins, glasses, and a half-gallon jug of milk.

"As the saying goes, 'all work and no play makes Jack a dull boy,'" he said.

"My saying is 'all work and no snacks makes Jordan a hungry boy,'" Jordan said. He grabbed a muffin and stuffed it into his mouth.

"So tell me about your visit to the school board," Mr. Duchesne said.

"It was great!" Catherine said enthusiastically. "I even got to quote George Polya."

Her dad chuckled. "One of my favorite mathematicians,"

A Knotty Problem

he said. "Let me guess, the one about finding an easier problem to solve?"

"That's the one," his daughter answered.

"Actually, the four of you could probably learn a lot from Polya's approach to problem-solving."

"Would you teach us?" Stephanie asked.

"Sure," he said. "Can I use the whiteboard?"

"He can't think without his white-board," Catherine joked.

Mr. Duchesne wrote as he talked. "George Polya took a very systematic approach to problem-solving. There are four steps. First, and maybe the most important, is to understand the problem. Second, you need to devise a plan for solving the problem. Third, carry out the plan. Fourth, and maybe the second most important, is to understand the result. In other words, what is the answer really telling me? Let me give you an example to show you how it works."

He wrote a problem on the white board:

> **If Tom has three times as many apples as Susan and Susan has one-fourth as many as Juan, who has four, how many does Tahmina have if she has two more than Tom?**

"Now I'm sure four smart kids like you could solve this in a minute or so, but let's use this easy problem to see the process. First, what is the problem statement?"

"How many apples does Tahmina have?" Justin ventured.

"Exactly!" Mr. Duchesne said. "This is important because sometimes we get so involved with the math that we forget what it is we are trying to solve."

"Yeah, I've definitely done that before," Jordan admitted.

"So let's start with the problem statement so we don't lose track of it." He wrote the first step on the whiteboard.

Tahmina =

"That's it?" Justin asked.

"That's it," Mr. Duchesne said. "It's what we are trying to solve, right? Actually, I'll add just a bit to it. Based on the problem, how many apples does Tahmina have?"

"Two more than Tom?" Stephanie asked.

"Right. Let's add that and I'll call that Plan 1."

Tahmina = *Tom* + 2   **Plan 1**

"That tells us that if we know how many apples Tom has, we can easily figure out how many apples Tahmina has. But we can't carry out Plan 1 because we don't know how many apples Tom has. So what's next?"

"Tom has three times as many apples as Susan," Stephanie said.

A Knotty Problem

"Perfect. Let's add that and call it Plan 2."

Tahmina = Tom + 2	**Plan 1**
Tom = 3 × Susan	**Plan 2**

"We can't carry out Plan 2 yet, can we?"

"No, because we need to know how many apples Susan has," Jordan said. "Let's see, she has one-fourth as many as Juan."

"That makes Plan 3," Mr. Duchesne said. He added that to the board.

Tahmina = Tom + 2	**Plan 1**
Tom = 3 × Susan	**Plan 2**
Susan = Juan ÷ 4	**Plan 3**

Before Mr. Duchesne could say anything, Catherine chimed in. "But we can't carry out Plan 3 because we need to know how many apples Juan has. That one's easy—he has four."

"Right. Let's add the last plan."

Tahmina = Tom + 2	**Plan 1**
Tom = 3 × Susan	**Plan 2**
Susan = Juan ÷ 4	**Plan 3**
Juan = 4	**Plan 4**

"Finally, a plan we can carry out," Mr. Duchesne said. "In fact, the plan is already carried out, right? Now, let's carry out the rest of the plans."

Tahmina = Tom + 2	Plan 1
Tom = 3 × Susan	Plan 2
Susan = Juan ÷ 4	Plan 3
Juan = 4	Plan 4
Susan = 1	**Carry out Plan 3**
Tom = 3	**Carry out Plan 2**
Tahmina = 5	**Carry out Plan 1**

"I love this," Justin said. "It just looks so organized."

"It is, Justin," Mr. Duchesne responded. "What I really like about it is that all solutions have the same look and feel. The words and symbols will change, maybe even the concepts, but the process of actually solving the problem will always be the same."

"Wow! That's really cool, Mr. Duchesne!" Stephanie said.

"Yeah, it's like you could solve any problem using this method," Catherine added.

Mr. Duchesne didn't immediately respond. He was staring intently at the whiteboard.

"Mr. Duchesne?" Stephanie said.

Still no response. Mr. Duchesne continued to stare at what he had written.

A Knotty Problem

"Dad?" Catherine said.

Mr. Duchesne nodded and smiled. He abruptly turned and started to walk out of the room.

"Dad? Is something wrong?" Catherine asked. Her dad stopped and turned around.

"No, my dear, something is right. Something is very right. I think I just might have solved my own problem." With that, he waved a hand and walked quickly out of the room, lost in his thoughts.

Chapter 12

"Hey Justin, can you do me a favor and water the hydrangea bushes?"

"Sure, Mom," Justin said.

Watering was one of those chores he didn't mind. It was mindless work, and he needed a break from his homework anyway. The Math Kids had spent the entire day on Saturday working on math problems in preparation for the district competition, and he had a three-page paper on the three branches of government to write that was due on Monday morning. Mr. Miller may have come around a little on math, but he still loved handing out writing assignments.

Justin was thinking about his paper as he reached for the hose coiled neatly in one corner of the back deck. He grabbed the end with the spray nozzle and started pulling the hose. He was halfway to the bushes when he came up short. Looking back, he saw the hose was hopelessly tangled. He spent the next ten minutes untwisting the hose, threading the spray nozzle in and out of loops, until

A Knotty Problem

he had enough hose to make it to the bushes. He turned on the water and began to water the bushes, careful to avoid directly spraying the large blue flowers.

While he watered, his thoughts shifted from his homework to the tangled hose. It reminded him of how he often found his video game controller cables tied into knots. He wondered if there was some logical explanation for why that happened. He was still watering and thinking about knots when he heard a familiar voice.

"Hey, Justin, what are you doing?" Jordan asked.

Justin looked up at his friend. "Practicing for the Olympic watering team," he said.

"Looking good. I'd suggest a little more arc on the water though. The judges love that."

Justin shook his head. "Instead of offering brilliant suggestions like that, how about helping and turning the water off."

Jordan turned the faucet to shut off the water. Justin walked the hose back to the deck. He looked at the tangled mess and shook his head.

"What's wrong?" Jordan asked.

"This stupid hose is all knotted up again. I unknotted it once already and now look at it."

"The same thing happens every year when my dad gets out the Christmas lights. It doesn't matter how carefully he packs them away. When he takes them out, they are always a mess."

"It's weird, isn't it?" Justin asked.

"Maybe," Jordan answered.

"Maybe?"

"I'm just wondering if there is a reason it happens. Maybe even something mathematical."

"I didn't think about that," Justin said. "If it's mathematical, I bet Catherine's dad would know something about it."

"Let's go ask him!" Jordan said excitedly. He loved talking math with Mr. Duchesne.

Justin thought about it. He really should be working on his paper, but he'd rather learn new math than write about boring government stuff.

"Okay, let's do it," he said.

A Knotty Problem

Ten minutes later, Jordan and Justin were knocking on Catherine's door. She looked surprised to see them.

"Hey, what's up?" she asked.

"We're actually here to see your dad," Jordan said. "Is he home?"

"Yeah, but he's been working in his office since yesterday afternoon. He barely stopped for dinner. I'm not even sure if he went to bed last night."

"Oh," Jordan said. "We don't want to bother him if he's busy. We just had some questions on knots."

"Knots?" Catherine asked.

"Like why they happen," Jordan added.

"It's not really important," Justin said. "It's just that I was trying to water the flowers this morning, and the hose was knotted. We were wondering if maybe there was some math behind cords and things getting all tangled up."

"Oh, there is definitely some math behind it," came a voice from across the room. Mr. Duchesne had overheard the conversation from his office and was now peeking out of the doorway.

"Hi, Mr. Duchesne," Justin said. "Sorry to bother you. Catherine said you were really busy, and..."

"No worries, Justin," Mr. Duchesne said. "I was ready for a break anyway."

"What are you working on?" Jordan asked.

"Oh, just an idea I've been kicking around. It's kind of

a problem-solver application," he said. "I made some good progress yesterday."

"Are you thinking it might really be possible?" Catherine asked.

"It's still a maybe," he said. "But it's looking more promising all the time. So you have some questions about knots?"

Jordan nodded. "I guess we're trying to figure out why cords and things get tangled up all the time. Is there some mathematical reason it happens?"

"I think the best answer to that question is yes and no."

"Yes and no?" Justin asked.

"The yes is that there is an area of mathematics called knot theory. It's been around for more than a hundred years."

"So it is mathematical," Jordan said.

"I suppose, but mathematicians look at knots in a very non-practical way. You see, if you have free ends of a string or rope, like tying your shoes, you can always untangle the knot completely. It might take some time and patience, but you can always unknot it. To a mathematician, that is not at all interesting. In math terms, a knot is always a closed loop. In other words, the ends of the rope are always joined so there are no loose ends. Here, let me show you."

He led them into the living room and drew a picture on the whiteboard.

A Knotty Problem

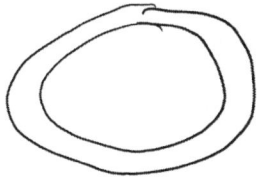

"This is what a mathematician would call a trivial knot, or sometimes an unknot."

"I'd call it a dough-knot," Jordan said.

"Of course you would," Justin said. "But if that's an unknot, what would they call a knot?"

"Great question. This is what is known as a trefoil knot." He drew another picture on the whiteboard.

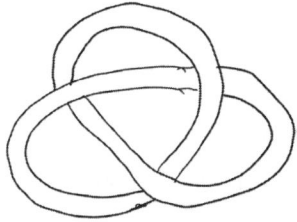

"I would call it a pretzel knot," Jordan said.

Mr. Duchesne smiled and shook his head. "You'll notice that there is no way to untie this knot. That makes it much more interesting to a mathematician," Mr. Duchesne explained. "With a knot like this, we can start to talk about characteristics such as knot crossings—this one has three crossings, for example—and even things like adding two knots together to make a third knot. Really interesting things."

"But none of that helps to solve our problem," Justin said. "I mean, it doesn't explain why the hose got all knotted up when I tried to water the flowers."

"No, it doesn't," Mr. Duchesne agreed. "And the topic of knots and tangles are definitely of interest. I mean, think of the hours people spend untangling hoses and necklaces and Christmas lights. But it's much more important than that. One example is in molecular biology."

"Biology?" Justin asked.

"Exactly. You've heard of DNA, right?"

"DNA is what carries all of the genes, isn't it?" Jordan said.

"Exactly," Mr. Duchesne said. "DNA is a molecule that has two strings that coil around each other. It controls the development, function, and reproduction of all organisms, including things like cancer."

"Where do knots fit in?" Justin asked.

"There are enzymes that change the topology of DNA, causing the strings to form knots. If we can create drugs that inhibit this knot tying, it can cause these cells to die. Drugs like this could be used to treat cancer or as antibiotics to fight infections."

"Maybe my dad should try an antibiotic on his Christmas lights," Jordan quipped.

Mr. Duchesne laughed. "I wish it were that easy, Jordan. Unfortunately, no one has really done much math around the issue of Christmas light tangling."

A Knotty Problem

"If math can't help, I guess we're out of luck, huh?" Jordan asked.

"Just because most mathematicians aren't looking at the problem of tangled Christmas lights, it doesn't mean that it's being completely ignored," Mr. Duchesne responded. "I read a study from a couple of physicists who did some experiments with putting ropes into boxes that were tumbled at different speeds. They found that complex knots sometimes formed in just seconds."

"Did they figure out why?" Catherine asked.

"No, but they did learn some interesting things with their experiment. They learned that the longer the rope was, the more likely it was to get tangled. But they also found that the smaller the box, the less likely the rope would get tangled. So, while it's not exactly an exact science, it does give us something to work with, right?"

"How does that help my dad with his Christmas lights?" Jordan asked.

"Well, he can start by making the string of lights shorter," Mr. Duchesne said.

"How does he do that?"

"Simple," Mr. Duchesne said, "tell him to connect the two ends of the lights together. It will make a loop, which should reduce the odds of tangling. It also cuts the length of the string of lights in half. Then have him put the lights into a tight box so they can't move around."

"That's genius," Jordan said. "Such a simple solution.

My dad is going to be excited to hear about this. Thanks, Mr. Duchesne!"

"Happy to help, Jordan."

"I do have one question," Justin said.

"What's that?"

"Well, you said you could always untie a knot if you have the ends free, but couldn't I make a really complex knot that would be impossible to untangle?"

"Ah, a Gordian knot," Mr. Duchesne said.

"What's a Gordian knot?" Catherine asked.

"Gordias was the king of Phrygia. Actually, his story is pretty interesting. You see, the Phrygians didn't have a king, but an oracle decreed that—"

"Sorry to interrupt, Dad," Catherine said, "but what's an oracle?"

"An oracle was a person who was said to be able to see into the future," Mr. Duchesne explained. "That meant when they said something, people usually listened. The oracle in this case said that the next man driving an oxcart into the city would become their king. So along comes Gordias, driving his oxcart. Boom! The next thing you know he's the new king. In gratitude, his son Midas dedicated the oxcart to one of the Phrygian gods and tied it to a post with an intricate knot. Another oracle said that anyone who could unravel the knot would become the ruler of all of Asia."

A Knotty Problem

"But surely someone untied the knot at some point, right?" Jordan asked. "I mean, you said that any knot with free ends could be untied."

"This must have been some knot," Mr. Duchesne said. "It was described in historical documents as several knots so tightly interwoven that it was impossible to see how they were connected. Anyway, years later the oxcart was still there, just waiting for someone to untie the knot. Along comes a man named Alexander. Like so many people before him, he tried to untie the knot. But, like the others, he failed."

"What did he do?" asked Catherine.

"Simple, old Alexander just pulled out his sword and sliced the knot in half."

"He cheated!" Justin exclaimed.

"You might say that," said Mr. Duchesne. "But I prefer to think that he simply changed the constraints of the problem. Alexander figured it made no difference *how* the knot was untied, just that it was untied. Out comes the sword—problem solved."

"And did he become the ruler of Asia?" Catherine asked.

"He did. He later went on to conquer most of Asia and became known as Alexander the Great."

"That's a cool story, Mr. Duchesne," Jordan said.

"If you ever hear someone talking about 'cutting the Gordian knot,' it's referring to this story. It means solving a difficult problem by changing the rules of the problem. By removing the constraints that made the problem difficult, it becomes easily solvable."

"Cutting the Gordian knot," Jordan said. "Hmm, I wonder..." His voice trailed off.

"Wonder what, Jordan?" Justin asked.

"Oh, nothing. I was just thinking about something."

Chapter 13

The following Friday Justin finally got the news he didn't want to hear. His dad had officially accepted the new role. There was nothing stopping them from moving to St. Louis now. He was going to call Jordan to tell him the bad news, but he remembered Jordan was out of town for the weekend.

Until the news, Justin had held out a slim hope that something could still change. Maybe his dad would find out something about the new company that would make him change his mind. Maybe the company would change their minds about his dad and offer the job to somebody else. Maybe, maybe, maybe—but all the maybes were gone now. It was a done deal. It wouldn't be long until all his stuff would be packed into boxes and thrown into a moving van. Justin and his parents would make the long drive halfway across the country to settle in a new house.

He would attend a new middle school in the fall, and he wouldn't know a soul. Everyone else would have tight friendships forged during six years of elementary school while he'd be starting completely over. He'd be the one standing alone in the hallway, invisible to the clusters of friends walking past him. They'd be complaining about their homework, discussing their plans for the weekend, and maybe even laughing at the "new weird kid" in third period English class. He wasn't like Stephanie, who had marched into their fourth-grade classroom and announced herself to the room. Justin knew he didn't have that kind of confidence.

Another thought crossed his mind: What if they didn't even have a math team? Or worse, what if they did but he wasn't good enough to make the team?

Faint rumbles of thunder sounded in the distance. Inside, Justin's mood was as dark as the storm clouds massing overhead.

***

Hundreds of miles away, the skies were clear, and Jordan was sitting in his Aunt Deja's kitchen. Deja was his mom's younger sister and his favorite aunt. She was always smiling, always took the time to listen to him, and most importantly, was a great cook. Jordan was digging into a plate of her skillet cornbread.

"How is it?" Deja asked.

Jordan had to swallow a large mouthful before he

A Knotty Problem

could answer. "It's like yellow squares of heaven," he said. "Soft, crumbly, sweet deliciousness."

Deja laughed. "You should do food reviews."

"And you should be on one of those cooking shows," Jordan said. He eyed the skillet and then looked up at his aunt.

She looked out the back window and saw Jordan's mom was still playing with Jordan's two younger cousins. Deja slid a spatula under another square of cornbread and slid it onto his plate. "Now don't you dare tell your mom I gave you another one."

"Mum's the word," Jordan said as he poured a large dollop of honey onto the cornbread.

"And how's my favorite nephew doing these days?" Deja asked.

"Not so great," Jordan said. He popped another forkful of cornbread into his mouth, using his tongue to get a dab of honey sticking to his bottom lip.

"Is there something wrong?" she asked.

"My friend Justin is moving to St. Louis," Jordan said. "He and I have been best friends since kindergarten. It's going to really stink not having him around anymore."

"That does stink," she said. "I remember when my best friend moved away. It's been thirteen years since she left, but I remember it like it was yesterday." She stared out the back window, a faraway look in her eye.

"How long had you been friends?"

"All my life."

"And what happened? Are you still friends?"

"Oh, we're still very good friends. I talk to her two or three times a week, in fact."

"But do you ever get to see her?"

Aunt Deja smiled. "I do. In fact, she's here visiting this weekend."

Jordan was confused but then he understood.

"You're talking about my mom, aren't you?"

"That's right," Deja said. "When she and your dad moved to Maynard, I thought it was the end of the world. Even though she is five years older than me, we were always very close."

"Why did they move?"

"Your dad got transferred. It couldn't have come at a worse time. Your mom was seven months pregnant with your sister at the time."

"Why didn't my mom just say no?"

"Your dad was the sole breadwinner at the time. Your mom was planning to stop working for a few years so she could raise the two of you. It was a good opportunity for your dad, so your mom went along with it. Sometimes we do things for our families even when it might not be the best thing for us personally."

"Yeah, that's why Justin is moving too," Jordan said. "His dad got a great job at some software company. I'm sure he'll be fine once he moves. It's just that…"

A Knotty Problem

"Just that what?"

"Well, I'm just worried that he'll forget about me."

"Will you forget about him?"

"No way. He's my best friend."

"Then you'll find a way to keep in touch," Deja said. "And when you get together, it will be like no time has passed."

"What do you mean?"

"You'll just pick up old conversations and it will be like he never left," she said. "That's the way it is with your mom and me."

"I guess, but it's going to be hard."

"It's a lot easier now than it was when your mom moved, especially with texting, video chats, social media, and all those other techie things. You're the smartest kid I know, and I think you'll figure out a way to make it work"

Jordan thought about those words while he finished up his cornbread, even licking the last of the honey off the plate while his aunt wasn't looking. Aunt Deja was probably right. He and Justin would always be friends, even if it became long-distance friends. But Jordan wanted something better than that.

He needed a plan, something that would fix everything. Justin was always the one that came up with the grand plans, some of them which seemed completely impossible—until they worked. *Now it's my turn*, Jordan thought. He reached for his phone and began tapping out a long text message.

Chapter 14

The clock was ticking. There were only three weeks until the state soccer tournament. There were only four weeks until the four friends would end their school years at McNair Elementary and compete in their final elementary school math competition. But the countdown timer weighing most heavily on everyone's mind was that there were only five weeks until Justin moved.

That time would go quickly because everyone was very busy.

At Justin's house, the packing had begun in earnest. The moving company had dropped off a huge pile of cardboard boxes and stacks of filled boxes were starting to fill the garage. Justin's mom had packed away the Christmas decorations, the photo albums, everyone's winter clothes, and the good set of dishes, the ones they only used for special occasions. Justin's dad had packed the camping gear and most of his tools, and he had taken down all

A Knotty Problem

the pictures from the walls. Justin had packed all the board games from the downstairs shelves. There were some he hadn't played in years, but his mom insisted that he put them all into boxes anyway. He suspected she was doing her best to keep him busy so he didn't spend all his time thinking about the upcoming move.

Stephanie's soccer team had moved to three practices a week in preparation for the state tournament. They practiced dribbling, shooting, passing, and defense. They did one-on-one defender drills. They worked on throw-ins, corner kicks, and shoot-outs. By the end of each practice, Stephanie was exhausted, but she had a smile on her face because it was a good exhaustion. She was in the best shape of her life and her team was ready to play.

With the semester coming to a close, Catherine's dad was spending a lot of extra time at the college. He was preparing final exams for eight different classes, holding extra tutoring sessions with students, and coaching graduate students on their individual projects. When he was at home, he was in his office working on his idea for a universal problem-solver application. His desk was cluttered with piles of computer printouts, stacks of math books, and at least a half dozen half-empty coffee cups. He had sticky notes stuck all over his walls, his computer screens, and even on the curtains. Catherine was doing her part by doing most of the house cleaning and meal preparation. She hoped her dad wasn't getting tired of macaroni and cheese, but he didn't seem to even notice what he was eating most nights.

Jordan was busy too, but no one had any clue what he was doing. Justin had tried to get ahold of him all week after school, but his mom kept saying he was in a meeting. *A meeting?* Justin thought. *What fifth grader is in a meeting? Who could he possibly be meeting with?* When Justin asked him at school, Jordan wouldn't say anything other than he was "working on a project." No word on what this project was or who he had mysteriously been meeting with. Catherine thought she had seen him once at the college when she took some dinner to her dad, but he hadn't turned around when she had called his name.

The only time the four had time to practice for the competition was during math time at school. They noticed that Mr. Miller had been giving them a little extra time to prepare. He had even found a book of math problems and each day brought a new set of challenges. On Wednesday, he handed a sheet of paper to Jordan. He had a little smile on his face.

"It's like he enjoys torturing us," Justin said.

"Nah, I think he's just trying to help get us ready for the competition," Jordan said. "Okay, let's see what he has for us today."

A Knotty Problem

He laid the problems on the desk so everyone could read them.

Stephanie looked over at the clock. "This is going to be a good test for us," she said. "We've only got fifteen minutes for these three problems. Let's divide these up. Catherine and I will take the first one. You guys take the second. The first team done can start on the third problem. Does that work for everyone?"

"That's how we always split up," Catherine said. "How about we switch it around this time? How about Jordan and I team up?"

There was an awkward silence as Stephanie and Justin looked at each other. Catherine looked on anxiously. She thought it would be good for Justin and Stephanie to work together, but she wasn't sure how Stephanie would take it. Finally, Stephanie nodded. Catherine breathed a silent sigh of relief. They split into pairs and started to work.

Wait! Do you want to try to solve these problems before the Math Kids do?

1. *X and Y are two different numbers from 1 to 50. What is the largest value that $\frac{X+Y}{X-Y}$ can have?*

(continued on next page)

2. The U-shaped figure contains 11 squares of the same size. The total area of the figure is 176 square inches. How many inches are in the perimeter of the figure?

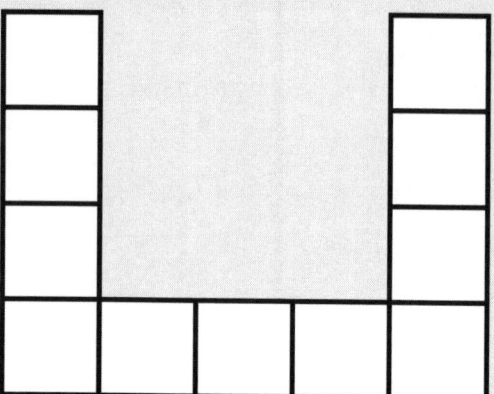

3. O is the sum of odd numbers from 1 to 99. E is the sum of even numbers from 2 to 98. Which is greater, O or E? And by how much?

At the back corner of the room, Justin and Stephanie examined the first problem.

"Okay, we're trying to find the largest value of this fraction," Justin said.

"That means we want the largest numerator and the smallest denominator," Stephanie said.

"That makes sense." A big grin came across Justin's face. "You ready to start on problem three?" he asked.

"What? You've already figured it out?"

A Knotty Problem

"I'm pretty sure. The largest numerator would just be 50 plus 49. The smallest denominator is 1, like 50 minus 49. That would make the fraction 99/1. The largest value would be 99."

"Can it really be that easy?" Stephanie asked in amazement.

"I think so," Justin said. "You just did a really good job of defining the problem. That made the math really easy."

"Cool, on to problem three!"

While they started on the third problem, Catherine and Jordan were just getting started on the second.

"This should be easy," Jordan said.

Catherine gave him a look. "You know we hate it when you say that, don't you?"

Jordan grinned. "Of course, I do. That's why I say it."

"In this case, I think you're right," Catherine said. "All we need to do is to find how big each square is and then it will be easy to find the length of the perimeter."

"I'm way ahead of you. The length of each square is four inches."

"How'd you get that so quickly?" Catherine asked.

"Simple. I just divided the total area of 176 by 11, the number of squares. That gives us 16, which is the area of each square. If the area of a square is 16 square inches, each side must be 4 inches. Easy peasy lemon squeezy."

"Great work. Now we just need to count the number of sides that make up the perimeter," Catherine said. She did a quick count and came up with 24. "And 24 times 4 inches is 96 inches."

"Done!" Jordan shouted.

Stephanie looked up from working on the last problem. "About time," she said. "Want to get over here and help?"

"It figures we'd get the tougher problem," Jordan said, drawing a look from Stephanie.

After rereading the problem, Jordan looked over at Stephanie. "This looks a lot like the first problem I ever saw you solve. Remember when you added up all the numbers from 1 to 100?"

"Mrs. Gouche sure wasn't happy about that, was she?" Justin said.

"No, she wasn't," agreed Stephanie. "You're right though. We should just be able to solve this one the same way."

On a sheet of paper, Stephanie lined up the odd numbers from 1 to 49. Underneath, she lined up the odd numbers from 99 to 51.

1	3	5	7	9	11	13	15	17	...	49
99	97	95	93	91	89	87	86	83	...	51
100	100	100	100	100	100	100	100	100	...	100

"If we add up each column, they will all equal 100," Stephanie said. "So 50 times 100 equals 5000."

A Knotty Problem

"That can't be right," Justin said.

"Why?" Stephanie asked, her voice a little snippy.

"Because there aren't fifty columns," Justin said. "There are only half that many since we are only counting every other number."

"Oh, that's right," Stephanie said. "Good catch, Justin. Okay, that means it will only be 25 times 100, so 2500 for the odd numbers."

"Let's do the same thing for even numbers," Catherine said. She used the same technique as Stephanie used, listing the even numbers from 2 to 48. Underneath that she wrote even numbers from 98 to 52.

2	4	6	8	10	12	14	16	18	...	48
98	96	94	92	90	88	86	84	82	...	52
100	100	100	100	100	100	100	100	100	...	100

"Okay, that gives us twenty-four columns with 100 in each column," Catherine said. "That gives us 24 times 100, or 2400."

"Don't forget the number 50," Jordan said. "It's not in any of the columns."

"That's right, Jordan," Stephanie said. "That means the even numbers add up to 2450."

"So the sum of the odd numbers is 50 more than the sum of the even numbers," Jordan said.

"Yeah," Justin said.

"You don't sound very happy about the answer, Justin," Stephanie said. "Did we get something wrong?"

"No, I think everything is right."

"Then what's wrong?"

"It's just that I think we might have been able to do this an easier way," Justin said.

"Really?" Stephanie said. "What are you thinking?"

"It was like your dad was saying, Catherine," he said. "It's important to really understand what it is we're trying to solve. The question didn't ask what the odd numbers or the even numbers added up to, just which one was bigger and by how much."

"And that's what we figured out," Stephanie said.

"We got there, but did we do it the easiest way?" Justin asked. "What do you think about this?" He drew two rows of numbers on the paper in his messy handwriting.

Odd	=	1	3	5	7	9	11	13 ...	99
Even	=	0	2	4	6	8	10	12 ...	98

"Now, if we subtract the even numbers from the odd numbers, we get 1 in each column," he explained.

Odd	=	1	3	5	7	9	11	13 ...	99
Even	=	0	2	4	6	8	10	12 ...	98
Odd − Even	=	1	1	1	1	1	1	1 ...	1

A Knotty Problem

"And 50 columns times 1 is 50, so the sum of the odd numbers is 50 more than the sum of the even numbers," Stephanie said in admiration. "We get to the same answer but much quicker."

"And that will be important when we've got a time limit for the problem-solving section," Catherine said. "Well done, Justin."

"Thanks," Justin said. "Well, really it's thanks to your dad for teaching us that understanding what the problem is asking is the most important step in the process."

Mr. Miller came by and looked at our answers. He consulted the answer sheet he had in his hand and nodded. "Not bad," he said. "All answers right with five minutes to spare. Nice work, Math Kids."

"Thanks, Mr. Miller," Jordan beamed. It was rare to get a compliment from their teacher, so he always appreciated it when he got one.

"When's the competition again?" Mr. Miller asked.

"Three weeks from this Saturday," Jordan said.

"Good luck. I'll try to stop by if I get a chance."

Stephanie's jaw dropped. Catherine looked like you could knock her over with a feather. Justin sank back in his chair and stared in disbelief. But it was Jordan's reaction that was the most comical. He looked like a dummy who was missing his ventriloquist. His mouth opened and closed like he was trying to say something, but no words came out.

Mr. Miller smiled and walked away.

Chapter 15

The next few weeks passed by quickly. Stephanie's soccer team practiced relentlessly. And when she wasn't on the soccer field, she was working on problems with the Math Kids. It was unusual for her to be able to walk home from school with Catherine on Friday afternoon. The day was warm and both girls were wearing shorts as they strolled leisurely down the sidewalk under the green canopy of leaves. Stephanie stopped several times as they were walking to do a couple of simple stretches.

"You doing okay, Stephanie?" Catherine asked.

"Fine, why?"

"Well, it's the day before the big tournament starts, and I figured that…"

"That what? I'd be a little scared?" Stephanie asked.

"Yeah, I guess. I know I'd be terrified."

"It's weird, but I feel perfectly calm. I don't know. When I'm on the soccer field, it just feels natural. I get so caught up in the game that I don't even think about winning or

A Knotty Problem

losing, just how to get that ball into the net. Now next week, at the district math competition, I'll be a nervous wreck," Stephanie said. "I guess it's because I know there will be other soccer tournaments, but..."

"I know what you mean," Catherine said. "Justin leaving means this will be the last time we'll be able to compete together as the Math Kids."

"I kind of have mixed feelings about that," Stephanie said. "I mean, I'd love to win but I'm still really mad at Justin."

"That's something I wanted to ask you about," Catherine said. "If you're so mad at him, why did you give him advice about moving?"

"Just because I'm mad at him doesn't mean he's not still my friend."

"He does make it hard sometimes though, doesn't he?

"He sure does," Stephanie said. "But I guess I'd still like to see us win together."

"It's only fair," Catherine said. "I mean, we've been through so much together. Kidnappers, international criminals, bullies..."

"And let's not forget Robbie's dad and, of course, Miller the Killer."

"You're right," Catherine said. "If we can make it through all of that, we won't let a few Mathketeers from Armstrong stand in our way next week."

"Mathketeers—I hate cutesy names like that," Stephanie said. "Let's kick their butts."

As they neared Catherine's house, they saw Jordan stepping down off of her porch.

"Hey, Jordan," Catherine said. "I thought you were at a dentist appointment."

"Um, it got canceled," he stammered. He quickly stuffed a few papers in his backpack before they could see what was written on them.

"Were you looking for me?" Catherine asked.

"No," he answered quickly. "Just, um, asking your dad a couple more questions about knots."

"Oh," Catherine responded. "Want to come in for a snack?"

"No, I've got to run," Jordan said, already heading down the sidewalk.

The girls watched as he walked quickly away. "That's unusual, isn't it?" Stephanie asked.

"That he had a question for my dad?"

"No, that he turned down a snack."

"Don't you think he's been acting a little weird lately?" Catherine asked.

"Now that you mention it, he has been a little secretive lately."

"Maybe he's just sad about Justin leaving," Catherine said.

"Yeah, that's probably it."

"Speaking of Justin, I invited him to the soccer

A Knotty Problem

tournament tomorrow," Catherine said. "I hope that's okay with you."

Stephanie shrugged her shoulders. "Doesn't matter to me one way or another," she said. "He hates soccer, so he probably won't show up anyway."

Chapter 16

The next day was sunny and beautiful, without a cloud in the sky. Jordan, Justin, and Catherine were on the sideline as Stephanie's team took the field for their first game. Justin wasn't sure how welcome he would be, but he didn't want to miss one of his few remaining chances to hang out with his friends. Stephanie raised an eyebrow when she saw Justin, but she smiled and waved to her friends as she did a few final stretches. She was relaxed and looked like she was having fun.

When the whistle blew, though, she put her game face on and went to work. The other team never knew what hit them. Stephanie was a whirling dervish, cutting in between players, handling the ball like it was on a string. Her passes were crisp and accurate, and her shots found the back of the net time and time again. When the final whistle blew, her team had won by nine goals. Stephanie was, without a doubt, the star of the game.

"I told you she was amazing," Catherine said.

A Knotty Problem

"Wow!" Jordan said. "I knew she was good, but I've never seen her play that well before."

Even Justin was impressed, and he usually didn't care anything about sports unless it was basketball.

There was a two-hour break before the next game. Catherine, Jordan, and Justin relaxed under a shady elm tree, munching on the snacks Catherine had brought and talking about their favorite subject—math. Stephanie spent her time with her teammates and coach, eating orange slices for energy while plotting strategy for the next team. They, too, had run over their opponents, so it was shaping up to be a high scoring match. As it turned out, it was high scoring, but only by Stephanie's team. The defense shut down the other team, only allowing two goals. Sydney was superb in goal, stopping thirteen shots, two of them with diving blocks. Stephanie's team won seven to two. They were into the quarter-finals. If they won their next game, they would be in the final four. The tournament was getting interesting now, and even Justin was following every bit of action in each game.

The third game was tight. Stephanie was double-teamed, sometimes even triple-teamed, whenever she got close to the ball. The strategy worked, and the teams went into halftime with a score of zero to zero.

"Okay, we expected this to happen, right?" Coach Clark said. "Their strategy is working, so we're going to change ours a bit this second half. Stephanie, I'm going to move you from center to left forward. If they double-team you like they have been, it should open up the right side. Riley, I need you and Maria to flood that side."

"You've got it, Dad," Riley said. "Oops, I mean coach. Coach Dad."

Everyone on the team laughed. Riley was always good for breaking up a tense situation with some kind of joke.

The second half started with a misplay by Maria that resulted in a breakaway for the other team. With no defender back to cover her, the opposing forward easily shot the ball past Sydney for a one to nothing lead. Two minutes later, Stephanie's team struck back. With two defenders on Stephanie on the left side, she managed to get off a pass to the center. Christiana immediately dumped the ball onto the right side, and Maria and Riley took it from there, cruising past the defense for a goal. The score was tied.

The coach's new strategy paid off again a short time later. Another pass to the right side and another goal by Riley. She strutted back to center field.

"Do you know what time it is?" she asked her teammates. "It's Riley time!"

Now the other team wasn't quite sure what to do. They shifted a defender to the right side, but that meant Stephanie only had one defender on the left. The next time she got the ball, she faked one direction, ran the other, and easily scored. They tried double-teaming

A Knotty Problem

Stephanie on the left and Riley on the right, but that left Maria unguarded in the middle. She scored twice unopposed. As the game neared its conclusion, Stephanie's team was ahead five to one.

And then disaster struck.

Stephanie had the ball and cut right toward the middle of the field. At the same time, Maria cut left to elude her defender. The two girls collided, their heads crashing into each other with a horrible thud. Maria managed to stay on her feet, but Stephanie crashed to the ground. When the coach reached her, Stephanie's head was covered in blood from a nasty looking cut across her forehead.

"Someone get a medic!" the coach shouted. Players from both sides looked on in shocked silence as a paramedic rushed onto the field. He held a towel firmly against her head to staunch the bleeding.

"What's her name?" the paramedic asked.

"Stephanie," replied the coach.

Leaning over the fallen girl, the paramedic asked in a loud voice, "Stephanie! Can you hear me?" Her eyes remained closed. "Stephanie!" Still no response. He waved to the other paramedic to bring the stretcher.

Maria was in tears as she watched her teammate. "I didn't see her," she said. "I didn't see her."

"It's not your fault," her coach consoled her.

"Is she going to be alright?"

"She'll be fine," he said.

"Are you sure?" she asked.

"I'm sure," he said. But the look on his face said something else entirely.

From the sidelines, Stephanie's friends looked on anxiously. Catherine's face had gone pasty white with fear. They wanted to rush out onto the field to help, but they knew they needed to let the medic do his work.

Stephanie had regained consciousness by the time the stretcher arrived, but her eyes were still glassy. The two paramedics gently lifted her onto the stretcher. They rolled her to the ambulance waiting nearby and loaded the stretcher aboard. Its siren wailing, the ambulance sped out of the athletic complex, leaving Stephanie's friends to watch after it through tears. "Please let her be okay," Catherine said over and over again, not even realizing she was speaking out loud.

With only two minutes left and Stephanie's team leading by six, the two coaches agreed to call the rest of the game. Stephanie's team was through to the final four, but a huge question remained: Would their star be able to play?

Chapter 17

Catherine, Jordan, and Justin sat together on uncomfortable green plastic chairs in the hospital emergency room waiting area. Catherine's eyes were red from crying. Jordan and Justin were uncharacteristically quiet. The three, along with Coach Clark and Stephanie's entire soccer team, had been at the hospital for more than two hours. During that time there had been no updates on Stephanie's condition. Her mom and dad had been allowed in to see their daughter, but that had been more than an hour ago.

Mr. Lewis came out and shared a few quiet words with Coach Clark while everyone else looked on anxiously. The coach nodded and Stephanie's dad walked back through the large swinging doors marked *Authorized Entry Only*.

"How is she, Coach?" Sydney asked.

"She had to get a half dozen stitches and has a mild concussion, but she's going to be fine," Coach Clark said.

"My gosh! Just how hard *is* your head, Maria?" Riley asked. Maria blushed while everyone else roared with laughter. Justin and his friends sank into their chairs in relief.

"Is she going to be able to play tomorrow?" asked Sydney.

"I'm afraid not," the coach said. "There is a concussion protocol that we have to follow, and that means she's not eligible to play for at least forty-eight hours."

"But..." Riley started.

"Coach," interrupted Sydney. "If Stephanie can't play, then I don't think we should play either."

"And not just because she's our best player," Maria said. "It just wouldn't be right. We're a team, Coach."

"I understand your feelings," the coach said, "but let me ask you a question. What do you think Stephanie would say?"

There was a long silence. Finally, Catherine spoke up. "She'd want the team to play."

"I think she's right," he replied.

"I don't agree," Justin said.

"You don't?" the coach asked.

"No. Stephanie wouldn't want you to play." He paused for effect. "She'd want you to win!"

"Then let's go out there and win," Coach Clark said.

The team cheered and high-fived each other.

***

A Knotty Problem

Long after the coach and soccer team had left, Jordan, Catherine, and Justin remained behind, still waiting for a chance to see their friend. Finally, Mrs. Lewis poked her head through the door and saw they were still there.

"Thank goodness," she said. "I was hoping you three were still here. She's been asking about you."

"How is she?" Catherine asked anxiously.

"She's a little banged up and they're going to keep her overnight for observation, but I think she's going to be just fine."

Catherine started to cry again, but this time it was tears of relief. Jordan and Justin remained silent.

"Do you want to see her?" Mrs. Lewis asked.

"You bet we do!" Catherine said.

Mrs. Lewis led them through the doors and down several halls before they reached an elevator. Then it was up three floors and down another two hallways before they finally reached Stephanie's room. There was a dim light coming through the open doorway.

"It looks like the lights are off," Catherine said. "Do you think she's asleep?"

"No, she's just really sensitive to light right now, so we're keeping the overhead lights off," Mrs. Lewis said.

She led them into the room. Stephanie lay back on her hospital bed, a thick piece of gauze wrapped around her head.

"I look like a mummy, don't I?" Stephanie asked.

"A little bit," Jordan admitted.

"I got a few stitches in my head, but the doctor said it shouldn't leave a scar."

"Oh, I definitely would have gone for the scar," Jordan said. "Maybe a cool lightning bolt."

"Just ignore him, Stephanie. How are you feeling?" Catherine asked.

"Mostly it's just a headache," Stephanie said. "But it's really hard for me to focus my eyes. Everything seems blurry."

"The doctor said that should clear up by morning," Mrs. Lewis said.

A Knotty Problem

"I hope so," Stephanie said. "I've got some math problems I want to work on."

"How about we worry about that tomorrow?" her mom said. "Tonight, I think you should just get some sleep."

"Yeah, sleep sounds like a good idea," Stephanie said. "But I wanted to see you first."

"What do you need, Stephanie?" Catherine asked.

"Nothing, just wanted to let you know that I'm going to be fine and not to worry about the district math competition next weekend. I'll be good to go."

"Never a doubt in my mind," Jordan said. "It would take more than the world's hardest head to stop you from helping us beat Armstrong on Saturday."

"You got that right," she said, her voice sounding very sleepy.

"We should let you get some rest," Catherine said.

Catherine and Jordan walked into the hallway, but Justin stayed behind.

"You need something, Justin?" Stephanie asked.

"I just wanted to tell you how great you were today," he said.

"Even though soccer is a stupid game, right?"

Justin winced slightly at her jab. "I mean, I knew you were good, but I guess I never realized how much your team depends on you."

"It's a team. That's what teams do," Stephanie said.

"I know, and I guess I got mad that your soccer team was more important than your Math Kids team. I guess I got a little jealous."

"But you—"

"Please, let me finish, or I might never get this out," Justin said. "When I saw you get hurt today, I wasn't worried about whether or not you were going to be in the math competition next week."

"You weren't?"

"Well, I guess I was, but that wasn't the first thing that went through my head. What I was most worried about was that one of my best friends was hurt."

"I'm one of your best friends, huh?" Stephanie asked.

"Of course," Justin said. "And I'm sorry I forgot that for a little while. I mean, the Math Kids are pretty important to me, but it's more than a math club, you know? I was glad we were able to solve problems under our truce, but I guess that's not what we're all about. I mean, we are, or were, a group of really good friends, and that's the most important thing. So I guess I'm just trying to say that I'm really sorry about the way I acted."

"Does that mean I'm back in the Math Kids?"

"I never should have thrown you out in the first place," Justin said. "You can come back in. You can even be president if you want."

"But Jordan's the president," Stephanie said.

A Knotty Problem

"Oh, I've been planning a coup for some time now." Justin smiled.

"You're a goof, you know that?"

"Yeah, I've known that for a while," he said. "Okay, I'd better get going so you can get some sleep."

"Thanks, Justin," Stephanie said.

"No, thank you," he said as he slipped out of the room.

Chapter 18

On Sunday morning, Coach Clark called the hospital and let Stephanie know her team had won their first game and had made it to the finals.

"Sydney was amazing," he said. "She stopped twenty-two shots. It was like she knew where the ball was going before they even took the shot."

"What was the final score?" Stephanie asked.

"Two to nothing," he said. "Pretty low scoring. We definitely missed you."

"Sorry, Coach."

"How are you feeling this morning?" he asked.

"A lot better. My head still hurts but at least my eyes aren't all fuzzy anymore."

"That's good to hear. When are they going to let you go home?"

"Pretty soon, I think," Stephanie said. "My parents are talking to the doctor right now."

A Knotty Problem

"Well, you're always welcome to come by and watch the final. We play at one-thirty."

"You know I'll be there if I can," Stephanie said. "If not, tell everyone I told them good luck, okay?"

Stephanie was released from the hospital a little after noon. It took a little convincing, but she talked her parents into taking her by the soccer fields.

"Just for a little while, okay?" her mom said.

"Sure, I just want to root them on," Stephanie said.

"Are you sure you feel up to it?" Mr. Lewis asked.

"Yeah, but you could do me one favor."

"What's that?"

"Can we drive by someplace that sells sunglasses?" Stephanie asked. "I guess my eyes are still a little sensitive to the light."

Her dad picked up a pair of cheap sunglasses at a drugstore near the athletic complex.

"Really, bright pink?" Stephanie asked him.

"Hey, it's all they had," he protested.

With her bandaged head and neon pink sunglasses, Stephanie was quite a sight to see as she walked across the field. Maria was the first to see her. She immediately began running in Stephanie's direction, followed closely by the rest of the team.

"Be careful, Maria," Riley shouted. "She's got a soft head, you know."

Maria stopped short of Stephanie and looked at her anxiously. "Are you okay?" she asked.

"Never better," said Stephanie. "Well, that's not quite true, but I'm doing fine."

"So what's the deal with those hideous sunglasses?" Riley asked.

"I'm just going incognito to keep my fans away," Stephanie said.

"Hmm, maybe I should get a pair of ugly shades," Riley answered.

"Who says you have fans?" Maria asked. Riley stuck out her tongue but then smiled.

"Oh, I have fans, trust me," she said.

"Hey, can we play a little soccer over here?" Coach Clark called. "The game's about to start."

"Good luck!" Stephanie shouted as they ran back to the field.

Stephanie walked to the sidelines. She was surprised to see Justin, Jordan, and Catherine.

"What are you doing here?" she asked.

"Um, you know how much I love a good soccer game," Justin replied.

"Yeah, right," Stephanie said.

"Actually, it's a lot more fun than I thought. I guess I'm starting to appreciate the game. A little."

"Well, I'm glad you came," Stephanie said. "It's good to have us all together again."

A Knotty Problem

It was a tight game, a seesaw battle from the beginning. Stephanie's team broke on top first with a goal by Maria, but the other team quickly countered with two of their own. Then Riley found the left side of the net to tie it up. Sydney made a diving save just before the halftime whistle sounded. It was all knotted up at two to two as they gathered around their coach.

"Okay, it's a tough battle out there, but you're doing great. Defense, they're getting too much space to maneuver out in front. I want you to drop back about ten yards to bunch them up a little. Offense, keep things spread out. Look for the open person and keep the ball moving at all times."

The team nodded. Stephanie, standing just behind her teammates, raised her hand.

"You have something you want to add, Stephanie?"

"Yes, Coach. I noticed that number twenty-two can't defend to her left. I think Riley could get around her on that side every time."

"Great observation, Stephanie. Anything else you're seeing out there?"

"Number fifteen, the tall one with the red hair, always drives to the right. I think Asha could over-defend her on that side and maybe get some steals."

"You know what I think?" the coach smiled. "I think I'm about to lose my job."

"No way, Coach," Stephanie protested. "I want to play."

"I know you do, Stephanie," he said. "Okay, who else is ready to play?"

They took the field for the second half. The other team

A Knotty Problem

moved carefully down the field. They passed back and forth, looking for an opening. Finally, the tall redhead cut toward the goal. Asha waited for her to make her move, then cut to her left. It was a risky move since it opened up the center of the field, but Stephanie's advice was on the money. Asha was right where she needed to be. She extended her left foot, kicked the ball free, and Stephanie's team was quickly moving upfield. Maria kicked the ball to Riley, who swept around the right side of number twenty-two and scored.

The coach looked over at Stephanie and smiled. "Are you sure you don't want to try coaching?" Stephanie just grinned, happy to be helping her team in whatever way she could.

With less than a minute or so to play, the score was tied at four. Maria took a shot, but it was easily saved by the opposing goalie, who kicked the ball down the right sideline. Asha went over to defend but fell as her feet got tangled up with a player from the other team. Now the other team had a two on one advantage. Moving down the right side of the field, they spread out to open up space. As the defender moved in, there was a sharp pass to the open player. Only Sydney stood in the way now. The shot was perfect, just out of reach of her diving attempt to block it.

The whistle blew. The game was over. The other team cheered as they realized they were the new state champions. Stephanie's teammates lined up and walked past the line of their opponents, shaking their hands and congratulating them, all while trying to hold back tears. They had come so close, only to lose on a last-second shot.

They gathered around their coach, several girls openly crying now.

"It's all my fault," Asha said. "If I hadn't fallen down, I would have been there to help."

"It wouldn't have mattered if I hadn't hit the post on two of my shots," Riley said.

"Hey, hey, hey," said Coach Clark. "It's not anybody's fault, and you have absolutely nothing to be ashamed of here. Think about what you accomplished this weekend. This team has never even been invited to this tournament, and you almost won the whole thing. That's amazing. Everybody played great. We just caught a bad break on that last play."

"Yeah, but—" Riley started before being interrupted by her dad.

"No buts. We'll get 'em next year."

"Now what do you say we continue this conversation over ice cream?" Coach Clark said. "You going to join us, Assistant Coach Lewis?" He looked over at Stephanie and smiled.

"You bet!" she said.

Chapter 19

Jordan, Justin, and Catherine were starting to get worried. It was Thursday morning, only two days before the district math competition, and Stephanie still wasn't back at school.

"I talked to her last night and she said she was feeling better," Catherine said.

"Do you think she had a relapse?" Jordan asked.

"I hope not," Catherine replied. "She said her vision was doing fine and the headaches were mostly gone, but I guess she still wasn't feeling up to coming to school."

"Do you think she'll be able to go to the competition?" Justin asked.

"I sure hope so," Catherine said. "If not, are we out?"

"I know we're supposed to compete in teams of four, but maybe they'll let us do it with just three," Jordan said.

"Do you think we need a backup plan in case she can't make it?" Justin asked. "Maybe we could get Joe Christian, or…"

"It's too late for that," Jordan said. "We've already submitted our team roster."

"Then what are we going to do?" Justin asked.

"Do about what?" came a voice behind them. They whirled around and there was Stephanie. Her head wrap had been replaced with an adhesive bandage. She looked paler than normal, but the smile on her face was all Stephanie.

"You're back!" Catherine shouted.

"Of course," Stephanie said. "I told you I wouldn't miss the competition, didn't I?"

"Yeah, but then you didn't come to school for three days," Justin said.

"It was those stupid headaches," she said. "I'd feel fine for a while and then—BAM!—another one would come along. But it's been twenty-four hours since the last one, so I talked my mom and dad into letting me come to school today."

"Well, it's great to have you back," Catherine said.

"It's great to be back. It was getting pretty boring sitting in a dark room by myself."

"I'll bet," Jordan said. "Unless, of course, you were watching movies all day and eating popcorn—then I guess it wouldn't be so bad."

"Let's get to some math," Stephanie said. "I've got a doctor's appointment at two-thirty, so I don't have a lot of time."

A Knotty Problem

Stephanie seemed back to normal. The Math Kids spent the next two hours working through problems in the library. They had talked Mr. Miller into letting them skip Social Studies and English, but they knew there would probably be some extra assignments waiting for them.

The lunch bell rang, and Justin looked up in surprise. "Already?" he said. "But we just got started."

"It's been two hours," Catherine pointed out.

"Yeah, but that's not enough," Justin complained.

"It'll have to be," Jordan said. "I'm starving."

"But the competition is in two days," Justin persisted. "Two days."

"Well, I have two words for you," Jordan said. "Chocolate brownies."

"Your mom's chocolate brownies?"

"Yep."

"With the caramel swirls?"

"Would they be my mom's chocolate brownies without the caramel swirls?"

"Did you bring enough for everyone?" Justin asked.

"Yes," Jordan answered.

That answer convinced Justin they had done enough math for the day.

***

On Friday morning, Justin waited on the sidewalk in front of Jordan's house. It was the last day of school, normally a day where he would look forward to a summer of video games, lazy afternoons floating in the municipal pool, endless days with no responsibilities, and most of all, no homework. But instead of this being the start of three months of freedom, it was the end—the end of his time at McNair Elementary, the end of his time in Maynard, the end of the Math Kids, the end of his friendship with Jordan, basically the end of everything he had ever known.

With those dismal thoughts clouding his head, Justin didn't even notice Jordan coming out of his house. He was startled by his friend's loud greeting.

"Wow, you sure are jumpy today," Jordan said.

"Sorry, I guess I was just thinking about some stuff."

"Last day of school. You ready for that?"

"It will be weird," Justin answered. "It's the only school I've ever known."

"Yeah, me too," Jordan said. "We did have some good times there, though, didn't we?"

Justin smiled as he thought back. "Remember in first grade when Bobby Cavillo put that garter snake in Mrs. Binford's desk drawer?"

"I've never heard someone scream that loud in my life," Jordan said.

"And I've never seen an old lady jump up on a desk like that."

A Knotty Problem

"Lebron James wishes he had her vertical leap."

They went back and forth with memories of their time at McNair Elementary as they walked to school: their run-ins with Robbie Colson and the other bullies, Stephanie's first day of class and her bet with Mrs. Gouche, solving the case of the burglars who had been using prime numbers to make it look like they were randomly robbing houses, becoming friends with Catherine and rescuing her father from kidnappers, helping Old Mike get his janitor job back when he was falsely accused of stealing from student lockers, winning the fourth-grade math competition...

As they neared the school, they ran into Catherine and Stephanie.

"Good morning!" Stephanie called out.

"It's hard to believe it's already the last day of school," Catherine said.

"Like really the last day of school in this case," Jordan said.

"That's okay," Catherine said. "After six years here, I'm ready to move on to Tyler Middle School for sixth grade. It'll be different, but we'll all be..." Her voice trailed off as she realized what she was about to say wasn't correct. She had intended to say they would all be together, but it wasn't true. Justin wouldn't be there.

"I'm sorry, Justin," she said. "I forgot that—"

David Cole

"It's okay, Catherine," Justin said. "I'm still getting used to the idea myself."

"When do you leave?" Stephanie asked.

"A week from today. The movers are supposed to get there first thing in the morning, and they said everything should be loaded by late afternoon. After that, I guess we're hopping in the car and heading out."

"Are you driving straight through to St. Louis?" Catherine asked.

"No, we'll probably stop at a hotel on Friday night and then drive the rest of the way on Saturday."

"My dad said St. Louis has a really good baseball team," Stephanie said. "Do you think you'll be able to go to some games?"

A Knotty Problem

"I'm not really into baseball," Justin said glumly. "And they don't have a basketball team."

"But they do have a—" Catherine started.

"I know. A great children's museum, a great science center, a hockey team, and the St. Louis Arch," Justin said. "That's all I've heard since my dad first mentioned the new job. Look, I'm sure St. Louis is a great town, but that doesn't really change anything for me."

"Well, maybe—" Jordan began before Justin cut him off.

"There are no maybes, Jordan," he said. "We're leaving in a week and that's that." Justin walked into the school without another word.

"I'm not so sure about that," Jordan said to himself.

Chapter 20

"This is already better than last year," Stephanie said as they stepped into the gymnasium at Maynard High School the next morning.

"Better how?" Catherine asked.

"Don't you remember? It was pouring down rain and the door to the gym was locked."

"Oh yeah, we got soaked, didn't we?"

"I remember it was a waste of a good bath that morning," Jordan said.

"Well, we may be dry, but we still have to face off against Armstrong," Justin said. "Speak of the devil…"

"We meet again." Josh Benson, the captain of the Armstrong team, came striding toward the Math Kids, a smile on his face. "I'm glad you could make it."

"Well, we have you at least partially to thank for that," Justin said.

"Happy to help. If we're going to win this again—and we will—I want it to be against the best competition."

A Knotty Problem

"Then it's a good thing we're here," Jordan said.

"Good luck," Josh said.

"Yeah, you too," Jordan replied.

Justin watched as Josh walked away, then turned to his teammates and asked, "Are we ready to do this?"

"Oh, we're ready," Stephanie said. "Revenge will be sweet."

They looked around the room. There were a lot of familiar faces, kids they had seen at the previous year's competition. There were a few new kids looking around nervously. The team from Armstrong, the one who trounced the Math Kids in the final head-to-head battle, was the same as last year.

"That's not good," Catherine said. "They were tough last year and now they have another year under their belt."

"Yeah," said Jordan. "But they might also be cocky and not take us seriously."

"Well, we'd better not do the same thing," Stephanie said. "Remember, we have to beat the other teams to just get into the finals."

"Good point," Justin said.

Mr. Trudeau, the head of the math department at the high school, was back for this year's competition. He got everyone settled into their seats and went over the ground rules. "It's the same format as last year," he explained. "The first round will be team problem-solving. Ten problems in one hour. The top two teams will face off in the head-to-head round for the district championship. Good luck, everyone!"

Just as they had in the previous year, the four broke into two teams. Stephanie and Catherine started with problem one and worked their way down. Jordan and Justin started at problem ten and worked their way up.

"Remember," Justin whispered. "Understand what the problem is asking before you start to solve it."

The bell sounded and the competition began. In just over forty-five minutes, the Math Kids had completed all ten problems, with each pair finishing five. With the remaining fifteen minutes, they switched problems and reviewed the work and solutions. When the bell rang again, they turned their problems in to the judges. Now the waiting began. Had they done enough to make the final round?

After an interminable wait, Mr. Trudeau finally made his way to the microphone. "Before I let you know which two teams made it into the final round..."

There was a round of good-natured boos from the kids who were already on the edge of their seats awaiting the results.

"I want you to know that this is the most correct answers I have ever seen in the problem-solving round," he continued. "Out of sixty total questions, the six teams

A Knotty Problem

correctly answered fifty-four of them. That means ninety percent of all problems were correctly solved, although I'm guessing that you all had already worked out the percentage in your heads, hadn't you?" There were a lot of nods among the students.

"And besides this being the most correctly solved problems, there were two teams that got all ten correct!" he said. "That's pretty amazing. Either we chose questions that were too easy"—more good natured boos—"or you are all getting too smart for us."

Justin, Jordan, and Catherine looked around nervously. Had they gotten all of their questions correct? If not, they were out of the competition. Only Stephanie looked confident, a small smile playing across her face. One hand absently touched her bandage to smooth down an edge.

"Okay, I've kept you waiting long enough," Mr. Trudeau said. "The first team going to the final is last year's returning champions—Armstrong Elementary!" The team quietly pumped their fists.

"They knew they had them all right," Jordan said. "They don't even look surprised."

"And the second team, also from last year's final..."

There was more, but that was all the Math Kids needed to hear. They were in the final, a rematch against Armstrong.

While they were setting up for the final round, Josh Benson strode confidently over to the table. "Nice work," he said, "although I'm sure you'll agree the problems were pretty easy this year. Now the fun begins."

"We're looking forward to it," Stephanie said.

"As they say, game on," Josh said.

"No, as they say, game over," Jordan replied.

"We'll see," Josh said with a smile. Before turning to return to his team, though, there was a moment where his confident look faltered.

"Okay, we're ready for the head-to-head final," Mr. Trudeau announced over the microphone. The Armstrong team marched confidently to their position. The Math Kids did the same.

"The first team to correctly answer seven questions will be the champions. Armstrong Mathketeers, are you ready?"

"One for all, and all for one!" Josh responded.

"McNair Math Kids, are you ready?"

"All for one, but one of us would be enough!" Justin responded loudly. The small crowd laughed.

"You've been saving that up for a year, haven't you?" Jordan whispered to his friend.

"You got that right," Justin whispered back.

> All the head-to-head competition questions, hints, and solutions can be found in the Appendix.

A Knotty Problem

The battle was on. For the first few minutes, it looked like Armstrong was going to repeat their rout of the Math Kids.

"If five negative numbers are multiplied together, is the product—"

Josh rang the bell without waiting for the question to be completed. "Negative!"

"Correct," Mr. Trudeau said. "The sum of the heights of Paul and Rachel is ninety-four inches. Rachel is eight inches taller than Paul. How tall is Paul?"

Josh rang in again. "Forty-three inches."

"Correct," Mr. Trudeau said. "The score is Armstrong two, McNair zero. Question three: A math test has ten problems. Five points are given for each correct answer and two points deducted for each incorrect answer. Roshan answered all ten questions and scored twenty-nine points. How many correct answers did he have?"

There was a long pause, but then the short redhead on Armstrong's team rang the bell. "He answered seven correctly," she said.

"That's right," Mr. Trudeau replied. "The score is Armstrong three, McNair zero."

The Armstrong team seemed invincible, and their confident looks said they knew it. Then, a mistake.

"A camera and case cost one hundred dollars," Mr. Trudeau said. "If the camera cost ninety dollars more than the case, how much does the case cost?"

The short redhead quickly rang the bell. "Ten dollars," she said confidently.

"I'm sorry, but that answer is incorrect," Mr. Trudeau said. "McNair, you will earn the point if you can answer correctly."

Stephanie rang the bell. "Five dollars," she said.

"That is correct. The score is now three to one. Question five: Six dollars were exchanged for nickels and dimes. The number of nickels was the same as the number of dimes. How many nickels were in the change?"

Justin rang the bell, just barely beating Josh. "Forty nickels," he said.

"Correct. That's three for Armstrong and two for McNair. Question six: There are six three-digit numbers that can be formed using each of the digits 4, 5, and 6 exactly once. What is the average of these six three-digit numbers?"

Catherine thought for a second and then rang the bell.

"No way she figured it out that quickly," Josh whispered to the boy on his right.

"Five hundred fifty-five," Catherine said confidently.

"Correct!" Mr. Trudeau answered. "That ties the score at three."

Josh looked up in astonishment.

From that point on, it was all McNair.

"One loaf of bread and six rolls cost one dollar and eighty cents. Two loaves of bread and four rolls cost

A Knotty Problem

two dollars and forty cents. How much does one loaf of bread cost?"

This time it was Jordan who rang the bell. "Ninety cents."

"Correct. Question eight: There are four large boxes. Inside each large box are three medium boxes. In each medium box, there are two small boxes. How many total boxes are there?"

Stephanie rang in and answered, "Forty."

"Correct again. The score is now McNair five and Armstrong three. Question nine: A baseball league has nine teams. During the season, each team plays three games with each of the other teams. What is the total number of games played?"

Both teams scribbled furiously on scratch paper. After a couple of minutes, Josh tentatively rang the bell. "Two hundred sixteen games."

"I'm sorry, that's incorrect," Mr. Trudeau said. "McNair?"

"One hundred eight," Stephanie said.

"Correct. The score is now McNair six and Armstrong three. Question ten: The average of five numbers is six. If one of the numbers is removed, the average of the remaining four numbers is seven. What number was removed?"

Catherine rang in as soon as Mr. Trudeau finished reading the question. "Two!"

Mr. Trudeau paused, then smiled. "That's correct, and

we have a new champion. Congratulations, McNair Elementary!"

The Math Kids high-fived each other. Josh and his team looked stunned as they solemnly lined up to congratulate their opponents.

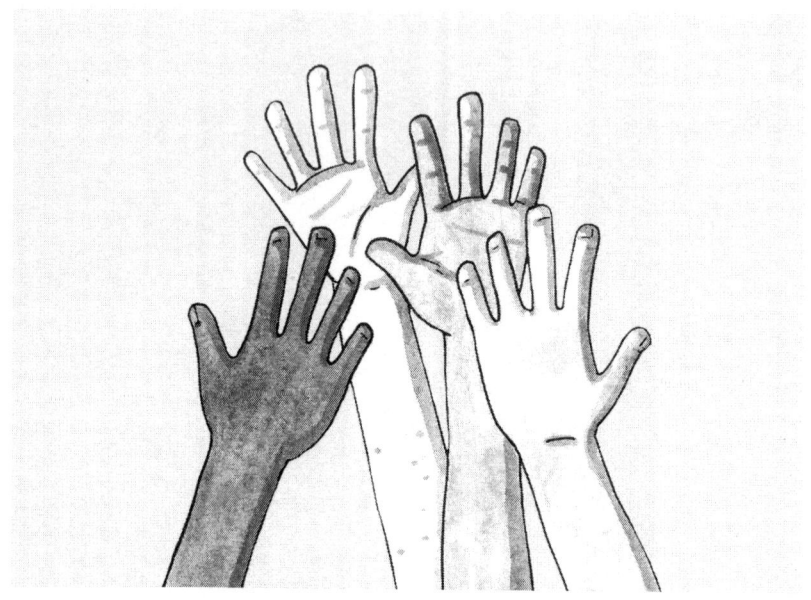

"Nice job, Math Kids," Josh said as he shook each of the winners' hands.

"Thanks, Josh. You definitely had us worried," Jordan said.

"I guess we'll be on the same team next year," Josh responded. "I look forward to that."

"Me too," Jordan said.

"Congratulations," came a voice from behind them.

A Knotty Problem

The Math Kids spun around to see Mr. Miller standing behind them.

"Mr. Miller?" Jordan said in surprise.

"I told you I'd try to stop by, didn't I?"

"Yeah, but..."

"I may not be as good a mathematician as the four of you, but I do keep my word."

"We appreciate you coming, Mr. Miller," Stephanie said. "It really means a lot."

"And we appreciate all the extra math time you gave us the last couple of weeks," Justin added. "You were a big reason we won this year."

"No, it was all you. You worked hard, and you earned this victory."

"Thanks, Mr. Miller," Catherine said.

"No, the thanks should go to you. It's not often I learn from my students. And no, I'm not talking about math, although I did pick up a little of that in the process. What I really learned is that a team is stronger than any of its members." Mr. Miller looked around to make sure no one else was in earshot. "Don't tell anyone else in class, but you were my favorite students this year."

"Wow. We may have to change your nickname," Jordan said. "What do you think about Miller the Chiller?"

"Don't you dare mess with my nickname!" Mr. Miller said. "To be honest, I kind of like the Miller the Killer thing. It helps me keep students in line."

"Okay," Stephanie laughed. "Your secret is safe with us."

Mr. Miller was still smiling as he walked away.

"Who's up for celebrating?" Justin asked.

"I'm sorry, but I can't," Jordan said.

"How come?"

"I've got a meeting I need to go to," he answered.

As Jordan quickly walked away, Justin called after him. "A meeting? Who are you meeting with?"

Jordan just kept walking as if he hadn't heard.

Chapter 21

Justin's going away party was the next day. His dad pulled the car into the park entrance and found a spot close to the pavilion they had reserved. Stephanie and her mom and dad and Catherine and her dad were already there and waved.

"Hey, Justin!" Stephanie called out enthusiastically. "Check out these decorations!"

Justin looked at the festive tablecloths on the picnic tables, the crepe paper streamers hanging from the pavilion, and the large sign reading *Good Luck!*

"Hi, Stephanie," Justin responded quietly. He was excited to see all his friends, but he wished it was for a different occasion.

It wasn't long before everyone else began arriving. Old Mike, the school janitor who had always had the Math Kids' backs, came in the old car he had been restoring since Jordan and Justin had first met him five years earlier.

"The car's looking good, Old Mike," Catherine said.

"Oh, I've still got quite a bit of work to do but I'm

getting there, little by little," he said. He ran a hand lovingly over the new hood he had just installed. "What should I do with this food?"

"Over on one of the picnic tables," Catherine said.

Special agent Carlson rode up on a shiny black motorcycle. "Cool wheels," Stephanie said.

"Thanks," Carlson said as he took off his helmet. "It was such a beautiful day that I couldn't resist taking out the bike."

Jordan's mom and dad arrived with Jordan's sister. Mr. Waters grabbed a cooler of soda from the trunk while Mrs. Waters carefully retrieved a large sheet cake from the back seat.

"What's the cake say?" Carlson asked.

"Sorry, it's top secret," Mrs. Waters said. "If I told you—"

"You'd have to kill me. I get it." The agent laughed.

"Wait, where's Jordan?" Justin asked.

"He'll be here soon," Mrs. Waters answered. "He said he had a meeting."

"Another meeting?" Justin asked. "Who is he having all of these meetings with?"

"I have no idea," Mrs. Waters said. "He just said he was at a meeting and would be here as soon as he could."

"That's weird," Justin said.

"I think he just wants to make a grand entrance," Mrs. Waters said.

A Knotty Problem

"Yeah, that sounds like Jordan," Justin admitted.

"In the meantime, let's get the grill fired up," Mr. Duchesne said.

"I brought my soccer ball," Stephanie said.

"What a shock!" Justin said. "Stephanie brought a soccer ball." He smiled to show he was only kidding with her.

Stephanie smiled back. "Who wants to kick the ball around?"

"No headers!" Stephanie's mom said.

"Got it, Mom," Stephanie said.

While the grownups started preparing food, the kids went out to the soccer field and were soon engaged in a spirited game of two-on-two soccer.

Thirty minutes later, the coals were hot, and the tantalizing smell of hamburgers drifted across the soccer field.

"Who's ready for some food?" Mr. Waters called out.

The kids came running from the field.

"Still no Jordan?" Justin asked.

"Not yet," said his mom.

"What is taking him so long?" Justin asked. "I can't believe he's missing my going away party." Jordan was his best friend. What could be more important than spending what little time they had left together?

"He'll be here," Mrs. Waters said.

"Yeah, whatever," Justin said.

Everyone had just filled their plates with burgers, chips, baked beans, and coleslaw when there was a strange thumping sound. Justin looked around. "What is that?" he asked.

"It sounds like it's coming from the trees on the other side of the soccer field," Stephanie said.

"It sounds like a helicopter," Agent Carlson said.

His guess was correct. A blue helicopter swooped low over the tops of the trees, circled once, then landed in the center of the soccer field.

"That looks like Mr. Howell's helicopter," Stephanie said loudly so she could be heard over the rotors, which were only now beginning to spin down. "Was he invited too?"

"I don't think so," Justin said.

The door to the helicopter opened and Justin was shocked to see Jordan climb carefully down to the ground.

"I told you, he loves making an entrance," said Jordan's mom with a grin.

Willard Howell followed Jordan, stepping lightly to the ground. Unlike his normal business suit, he was dressed in shorts, sandals, and a flowered Hawaiian shirt. He and Jordan walked together to the pavilion.

"What's going on here?" Justin asked.

"We just thought we'd drop in to your party," Jordan said. He was grinning ear to ear.

"Hi, Justin," Mr. Howell said. He nodded at Catherine's dad. "Afternoon, professor."

"Wait, how do you know my dad?" Catherine asked.

A Knotty Problem

"Let's just say we've done a little business together," Howell said. "Well, to be more accurate, we're about to do a little business together."

Catherine looked over at her dad. Mr. Duchesne tried to put on an innocent face, but he just couldn't pull it off. He broke into laughter.

"Tom, maybe you can explain," Mr. Howell said.

All eyes turned to Justin's dad. "I could, but I think the honor should really go to Jordan. This whole thing was his idea after all."

"Will someone just tell me what is going on here?" Justin pleaded.

Jordan stepped forward and took a deep breath. "I cut the Gordian knot," he said.

"What?"

"You remember Catherine's dad telling us about the knot? You know, the one that couldn't be untied."

"Yeah," Justin said, still unclear where this was leading.

"Well, he told us that Alexander the Great solved the knot problem by changing the constraints."

"Okay," Justin said, "But what does—"

"You see, I had this unsolvable problem," Jordan continued over Justin. "My best friend's dad found this great job in St. Louis. The problem was that there wasn't a job in Maynard that was as good as this new job. Well, I don't know anything about business, so it sure looked unsolvable to me."

"Okay," Justin said, still trying to figure out where Jordan was going.

"But then I remembered I knew someone who knew

A Knotty Problem

an awful lot about business," Jordan went on. "And, even better, he owed us one." At that comment, Mr. Howell smiled.

"So I went to Mr. Howell and asked him for help."

Mr. Howell stepped in at this point. "When Jordan came to me and asked if I could help, I told him no. I mean, I couldn't just create a new company based in Maynard just so Justin's dad wouldn't have to leave town."

"The knot remained tied," Jordan said. "That is, until I heard Catherine's dad talking about this great idea for creating an application that could solve problems. I thought maybe I could use his app to solve my own problem."

Mr. Duchesne stepped forward. "Unfortunately, the app wasn't ready yet. It was a good idea, but I had problems of my own. I didn't have the resources I needed to get my idea off the ground. I needed capital, software developers, and most of all, someone to manage the whole team."

"That's when it hit me," Jordan said. "What if I combined the problems into one problem. If I could solve Mr. Duchesne's problem, maybe it would also solve my problem."

"In other words," Mr. Duchesne said, "Jordan changed the constraints of the problem."

"So I went back to Mr. Howell," Jordan continued. "I told him about the application Mr. Duchesne was working on."

"It sounded like a winner to me," Howell said. "Jordan set up a meeting with the professor. After talking it over with him, it sounded like something I wanted to invest in."

"I still needed someone to take charge of the team though," Mr. Duchesne said.

"I guess that's where I came in," Justin's dad said. "Willard approached me about managing the team—"

"Not just the team, the whole company," Mr. Howell interrupted.

"Right, the whole company," Justin's dad said. "So, it turned out there *was* a company right here in Maynard that gave me an even better opportunity than the company in St. Louis."

"But what are you saying?" Justin asked, still confused.

"I'm going into business with Mr. Howell and Professor Duchesne," he said.

"But what about the company in St. Louis?" Justin asked. "Aren't they going to be mad?"

"Maybe, but this was an offer I couldn't refuse," his dad said.

"We're not moving to St. Louis?"

"No. We're staying right here in Maynard."

The next few minutes were chaotic. There were screams, dances of joy, handshakes, high fives, hugs, and shouted conversations. Justin had more questions, but they would have to wait for another day. The only thing that mattered was that he wasn't moving.

A Knotty Problem

"What are you going to call the company?" Stephanie asked when things calmed down.

"I think I can answer that," Jordan's mom said. She removed the lid of the cake. In bright blue frosting, there was a logo of a complicated knot next to the company name: G-Knot.

"Your idea, Jordan?" Stephanie asked.

"Well, it was the least they could do," Jordan said. "Well, that and another helicopter ride."

"Was I the only one who didn't know about this?" Justin asked.

"We didn't know," Stephanie and Catherine said together.

"It actually all came together this week," Howell explained. "We didn't want to say anything until we had worked out all the details."

"The house," Justin said. "What about the house? Everything is all packed up. Will we still have to move?"

"No, we were able to get out of the contract," his mom said. "All we'll have to do is unpack. Just think how clean the house will be!"

"Wait a minute," Justin replied. "Are you sure this wasn't all some elaborate scheme to get me to clean my room?"

"Oh, I'm sure it won't stay clean for long," his mom said, drawing laughter from everyone.

The End

Appendix

Order of Operations

In math, the order of operations is a set of rules that tell us the sequence in which the operations should be performed to solve an equation.

The order is:
1. **P**arentheses
2. **E**xponents and Roots
3. **M**ultiplication/**D**ivision
4. **A**ddition/**S**ubtraction

In the United States, this order is sometimes referred to as PEMDAS. Another way of remembering the order is by using the mnemonic "**P**lease **E**xcuse **M**y **D**ear **A**unt **S**ally."

Note that in some countries, the acronym used for the order of operations may be slightly different. In Canada and New Zealand, for example, the order of operations is referred to as BEDMAS (**B**rackets, **E**xponents, **D**ivision/ **M**ultiplication, **A**ddition/**S**ubtraction). Other countries use BODMAS (**B**rackets, **O**rders, **D**ivision/**M**ultiplication, **A**ddition/**S**ubtraction).

To use the order of operations, you would first do anything that is in parentheses or brackets, then evaluate any exponents or roots, then do any multiplication or division, then do any addition or subtraction. Note that multiplication and division are at the same level, so if an expression has both multiplication and division, we would evaluate them from left to right. The same holds true for addition and subtraction.

Here is an example:

$8 + (3 - 2) \times 4^2 \div 2$

(P)   First evaluate what is inside the parentheses.

$(3 - 2) = 1$, leaving us with $8 + 1 \times 4^2 \div 2$

(E)   Next, evaluate the exponent.

$4^2 = 16$, leaving us with $8 + 1 \times 16 \div 2$

(MD)   Next, do the multiplication and division from left to right.

$8 + 1 \times 16 \div 2$

$8 + 16 \div 2$

$8 + 8$

(AS)   Finally, do the addition and subtraction from left to right.

$8 + 8 = 16$

A Knotty Problem

What would happen if we ignored PEMDAS and just did everything from left to right?

$$8 + (3 - 2) \times 4^2 \div 2$$

$8 + 3$	→	$11 - 2 \times 4^2 \div 2$
$11 - 2$	→	$9 \times 4^2 \div 2$
4^2	→	$9 \times 16 \div 2$
9×16	→	$144 \div 2$
$144 \div 2$	→	72

We would get a very different answer! That's why it's important that we follow these rules so that everyone will get a consistent answer to the same expression.

Fermat's Last Theorem

When Catherine was addressing the school board, she mentioned Andrew Wiles and his proof of Fermat's Last Theorem. A theorem is a statement which has been proved by a logical argument called a proof.

Fermat's Last Theorem says that there are no positive integers a, b, and c that satisfy the equation

$a^n + b^n = c^n$, except where n = 1 or 2.

What does this mean?

First, a^n means to multiply a by itself n times. For

example, a^3 means to multiply a by itself three times. In other words, $a^3 = a \times a \times a$. In the simplest case, $a^1 = a$.

Fermat's Last Theorem says that we can find three numbers that satisfy $a^1 + b^1 = c^1$. One example is $1 + 2 = 3$.

Easy, right? There are infinite solutions to this.

The theorem also says we can find three numbers that satisfy the equation $a^2 + b^2 = c^2$. One example is $3^2 + 4^2 = 5^2$

But Fermat's Last Theorem says we can't find solutions for $a^3 + b^3 = c^3$ or $a^4 + b^4 = c^4$ or any number greater than 2.

The theorem was first stated by Pierre de Fermat around 1637. It was written in the margin of a book called *Arithmetica*. Fermat said he had a proof, but that it was too large to fit in the margin. It became known as Fermat's Last Theorem because all his other theorems were proved. It was 358 years before anyone was able to prove it. Andrew Wiles, an English mathematician, published a proof in 1995.

Before it was finally proved, Fermat's Last Theorem was listed in the *Guinness Book of World Records* as the "most difficult mathematical problem" because it had so many unsuccessful proofs.

The quote Catherine used when discussing Andrew Wiles was from an interview he did for the NOVA program. You can read that interview to learn more about Andrew Wiles and how he solved Fermat's Last Theorem: www.pbs.org/wgbh/nova/article/andrew-wiles-fermat/.

A Knotty Problem

George Polya

George Polya was a Hungarian mathematician. He taught at ETH Zurich in Switzerland from 1914 to 1940 and at Stanford University from 1940 to 1953. He became known as "the father of problem-solving" for his approach to math education. At the school board meeting, Catherine quotes from his book *How To Solve It*, which has been in print since 1945 and has sold over a million copies.

Gordian Knot

According to Greek legend, the story of Alexander the Great being challenged by the Gordian knot is true, although there are different versions of how he solved the problem. The popular account, as told by Mr. Duchesne in the book, is that he used his sword to cut the knot in half. Some classical scholars, however, believe it is more likely that he pulled the knot out of the pole pin, which exposed the two ends of the cord. Once he had the two ends free, he could untie the knot.

David Cole

District Math Competition Head-to-Head Questions

1. If five negative numbers are multiplied together, will the product be positive or negative?

    When two positive numbers are multiplied together, the product will always be a positive number. When two negative numbers are multiplied together, the product will also be a positive number. The only time the product will be negative is if a positive number is multiplied by a negative number.

    If there are an even number of negative numbers, the product will always be a positive number (two negatives multiplied together will be positive). If there are an odd number of negative numbers, the product will always be a negative number.

2. The sum of the heights of Paul and Rachel is ninety-four inches. Rachel is eight inches taller than Paul. How tall is Paul?

    Let's use P to represent Paul's height and R to represent Rachel's height. We know the sum of their heights is 94 inches. This gives us the equation

    $P + R = 94$

    We also know Rachel is 8 inches taller than Paul. If we write this as an equation, we get

    $R = P + 8$

A Knotty Problem

We can substitute the second equation into the first equation (instead of using R, we'll use P + 8). This gives us

P + (P + 8) = 94

Another way of writing this is

2P + 8 = 94

If we subtract 8 from both sides of the equation, we have

2P = 76

If we divide both sides of the equation by 2, we're left with

P = 38

So Paul is 38 inches tall.

Let's check our answer. Since Rachel is 8 inches taller than Paul, that means Rachel is 38 + 8 or 46 inches tall. That means the sum of their heights is 38 + 46 = 94 inches, which checks out!

3. *A math test has ten problems. Five points are given for each correct answer and two points deducted for each incorrect answer. Roshan answered all ten questions and scored twenty-nine points. How many correct answers did he have?*

Let's use C to represent a correct answer and W to represent a wrong answer. We know the total number of answers was 10, so we have

C + W = 10 (another way to write this is W = 10 − C)

We also know that Roshan scored a total of 29 points. If there are +5 points for every correct answer and −2 points for every wrong answer, that means

    $5C - 2W = 29$

If we substitute $(10 - C)$ for W in this equation, we get

    $5C - 2(10 - C) = 29$

To multiply −2 by (10 − C), we first multiply −2 by 10 to get −20. Then we multiply −2 by −C to get 2C (remember that multiplying two negative numbers will give us a positive product). Now we have

    $5C - 20 + 2C = 29$

If we combine the Cs together, we get

    $7C - 20 = 29$

If we add 20 to both sides of the equal sign, we get

    $7C = 49$

Dividing both sides by 7, we get

    $C = 7$

That means Roshan got 7 answers right (and 3 answers wrong). He got 35 points (5 × 7) for his correct answers and lost 6 points (3 × 2) for his incorrect answers. Since 35 − 6 = 29, our math checks out!

4. A *camera and case cost one hundred dollars. If the camera cost ninety dollars more than the case, how much does the case cost?*

A Knotty Problem

The Armstrong team made a common mistake on this problem. They subtracted 90 from 100 to get 10 for the cost of the case. Where did they go wrong?

If we use C to represent the cost of the camera and S to represent the cost of the case, we have

$$C + S = 100$$

If the camera cost 90 dollars, the case would be 10 dollars. But the problem says the camera *cost 90 dollars more than the case.*

If we write this down as an equation, it means

$$C = S + 90$$

Let's substitute (S + 90) for C in our first equation. We get

$$(S + 90) + S = 100$$

Another way of writing this is

$$2S + 90 = 100$$

After subtracting 90 from both sides, we have

$$2S = 10$$

Dividing both sides by 2, we find

$$S = 5$$

So the cost of the case is 5 dollars, not 10 like the Armstrong team answered.

Since the camera is 90 dollars more than the case, the camera cost 95 dollars. If we add 95 (the cost of the camera) to 5 (the cost of the case), we get 100 dollars, so our math checks out.

5. *Six dollars were exchanged for nickels and dimes. The number of nickels was the same as the number of dimes. How many nickels were in the change?*

   Let N be the number of nickels and D be the number of dimes. That gives us two equations:

       N = D   There are an equal number of nickels and dimes.

       5N + 10D = 600   Nickels are 5 cents and dimes are 10 cents. They must total 6 dollars, which is 600 cents.

   We can substitute N for D in the second equation to get

       5N + 10N = 600
       15N = 600
       N = 40

   That means there are 40 nickels (and 40 dimes). 40 nickels is 2 dollars and 40 dimes is 4 dollars, so they total 6 dollars.

6. *There are six three-digit numbers that can be formed using each of the digits 4, 5, and 6 exactly once. What is the average of these six three-digit numbers?*

   Let's start by finding all the three-digit numbers

A Knotty Problem

that can be formed using the digits 4, 5, and 6 exactly once.

456
465
546
564
645
654

We could calculate the average by simply adding these numbers together and dividing by 6 (the number of numbers), but Catherine answered this question very quickly in the story. Did she find a way to make it easier?

Look at the first column of numbers (the hundreds digit). You will notice there are two 4s, two 5s, and two 6s. Now look at the second column (the tens digit). Same story: two 4s, two 5s, and two 6s. Finally, look at the third column (the ones digit). Again, we'll find two 4s, two 5s, and two 6s.

If we average two 4s, two 5s, and two 6s, the average is 5. We can check this out by adding the numbers and dividing by 6.

(4 + 4 + 5 + 5 + 6 + 6) = 30 and 30 ÷ 6 = 5

Catherine recognized that each column would average to 5, so she was able to quickly give the final answer of 555.

7. One loaf of bread and six rolls cost one dollar and eighty cents. Two loaves of bread and four rolls cost two dollars and forty cents. How much does one loaf of bread cost?

Let B be the cost of a loaf of bread and R be the cost of a roll.

$B + 6R = 180$ (since $1.80 is the same as 180 cents)

Another way to write this equation is

$B = 180 - 6R$

We know that 2 loaves of bread and 4 rolls cost $2.40, or

$2B + 4R = 240$

Since we know $B = 180 - 6R$, we can substitute for B to get

$2(180 - 6R) + 4R = 240$

$360 - 12R + 4R = 240$

$360 - 8R = 240$

Adding 8R to both sides, we get

$360 = 240 + 8R$

Subtracting 240 from both sides, we get

$120 = 8R$

That means that each roll costs 15 cents ($120 \div 8$).

Since $B = 180 - 6R$, we can substitute for R to get

$B = 180 - 90 = 90$

Each loaf of bread is 90 cents.

A Knotty Problem

8. *There are four large boxes. Inside each large box are three medium boxes. In each medium box, there are two small boxes. How many total boxes are there?*

   There are three sizes of boxes. We can call them L (large), M (medium), and S (small).

   We know there are 4 large boxes, so L = 4.

   In each large box, there are 3 medium boxes, so M = 4 × 3 = 12.

   In each medium box, there are 2 small boxes, so S = 12 × 2 = 24.

   Now we just add L + M + S to get the total number of boxes.

   Total boxes = L + M + S
                          = 4 + 12 + 24
                          = 40

9. *A baseball league has nine teams. During the season, each team plays three games with each of the other teams. What is the total number of games played?*

   Each team plays 3 games each against the 8 other teams in the league. Since there are 9 teams, we just multiply 9 × 3 × 8 = 216.

   That was the answer given by Armstrong, but it wasn't right. Why? In each game, there are two teams playing. Stephanie recognized this, so she divided 216 by 2 to get the actual number of games played. Her answer of 108 was correct.

10. *The average of five numbers is six. If one of the numbers is removed, the average of the remaining four numbers is seven. What number was removed?*

Catherine was able to quickly answer this question. How did she do it so fast?

How do we calculate the average of a group of numbers? We first add up all the numbers to get the sum. Then we divide this by the size of the group.

Average = (sum of numbers) ÷ (size of group)

There's another way we can look at this equation. If we know the average and the size of the group (the number of numbers), we can easily calculate the sum.

Sum = Average × size of group

Catherine quickly figured out the sum of the numbers by multiplying the average (6) by the number of numbers (5) to get 30.

Now a number is removed from the group. The new average is seven. Catherine calculated the new sum.

New sum = new average × new size of group
New sum = 7 × 4
28 = 7 × 4

Since the original sum was 30 and the new sum is 28, the number removed had to have been the number 2.

Coming Next!

An Artificial Test

Book 8 in The Math Kids Series

by
David Cole

Chapter 1

"Okay, everyone, we're almost ready for takeoff, so it's time to get those seatbelts fastened," the pilot said over the loudspeaker.

"Wow, this jet is amazing," Stephanie Lewis exclaimed as she looked around at the beautiful teak wood, the thick blue carpet, and the subdued lighting.

"It's a Gulfstream G650ER," Justin Grant said from the seat behind her. "This baby can go more than seven hundred miles per hour and fly eighty-six hundred miles without refueling."

"What a shock," Catherine Duchesne said with fake surprise. "Justin read up on all of the jet stats before the trip."

"And I didn't even tell you the most important thing," he responded. "This jet cost more than sixty-six million dollars. Sixty. Six. Million. Dollars."

"That's not the most important thing," came the voice of Jordan Waters, Justin's best friend since kindergarten.

He was sitting across the aisle from Justin and was grinning from ear to ear. This was Jordan's first time on a plane, and the fact that it just happened to be on a custom-designed luxury business jet owned by billionaire Willard Howell was definitely an added plus.

"What's more important?" Justin asked.

"Whether or not they serve dinner on this plane."

Aimee, the flight attendant, overheard the conversation and answered. "Yes, there will most certainly be dinner. I believe Mr. Howell ordered up something special for you."

"It's not some fancy stuff, is it?" Justin asked anxiously. "You know, like snails or caviar or something like that?"

"What's caviar?" Jordan asked.

"Fish eggs," Justin said.

"Yuck!" Jordan said. "No fish eggs for me, please. And no green stuff like salad or brussels sprouts."

Aimee smiled. "I think you'll be happy with Mr. Howell's menu choices. How do hamburgers and french fries sound?"

"Now you're speaking my language," Jordan said.

"And I believe we have everything we need for hot fudge sundaes for dessert," Aimee said.

"Now you're *really* speaking my language!"

The four friends settled back into their plush leather seats, checked their seat belts, and looked out the window as the jet began to taxi out to the runway. They were going into sixth grade in the fall, but they had one

An Artificial Test

more special adventure before that happened, so school was the last thing on their minds.

It all started when Justin's dad was offered a new job that would have required the family to move to St. Louis. At the same time, Catherine's dad, a professor at the local university, had come up with an idea for an application that could solve complicated problems. Jordan was able to recognize that the two should be working together and contacted Mr. Howell to finance it. Mr. Howell had agreed and G-Knot, the new company, was off to a great start. Two months later, Mr. Grant and Mr. Duchesne were heading to London to demonstrate the initial version of the software with a potential customer. It was Mr. Howell's suggestion that the four kids join them on the trip.

"Are you sure?" Justin's dad had asked when Howell had brought it up.

"Why not?" the eccentric billionaire had asked. "Look, the Math Kids have proven themselves to be very capable. I think it's high time they get to put math aside for a couple of weeks and see the world. You can all fly over on my jet, and I'll meet you there in a week when I'm done with my meetings in New York."

The Math Kids was a club Justin, Jordan, and Stephanie had formed when they were in fourth grade. Catherine had joined when they needed another person for the district math competition. The club was originally created around the love they had for solving math problems, but it turned out their math skills were useful for solving real-world problems, too, including catching some neighborhood burglars, finding a fortune in lost gold, and rescuing Catherine's dad from kidnappers.

As soon as the decision for the kids to go was made, there was a flurry of activity—getting passports for everyone, booking hotels, and arranging for a guide for the kids. Now the kids, and Justin and Catherine's dads were all on a private jet headed to London, England.

"We've been cleared for takeoff," the pilot said.

"Here we go," Jordan said, his fingers tightening on the armrests. The engines roared and the jet sped down the runway and soared quickly into the evening sky. Everyone stared out of the windows as the houses grew smaller and smaller. Soon everything was lost to sight as the jet passed through a bank of clouds. Justin pulled a small book out of his overstuffed backpack and began thumbing through the pages.

"You brought a book?" Jordan asked incredulously. It was summertime and Justin was not much of a reader even when they were in school.

"It's a language translation guide," Justin said.

"You do know they speak English in England, don't you?" Stephanie teased.

"Yeah, but not the same English we speak," he said. "For example, what we call chips in the United States are called crisps in England. If you ask for chips over there,

An Artificial Test

you'll get something like French fries—you know, like fish and chips? And a biscuit over there is what we would call a cookie."

"Interesting," Stephanie said. "Does your little book have any translations other than food?"

"It sure does. Here's one for you. What we call soccer—you know, that game you play all the time—the English call that football. Not at all like the *real* football we have in the States."

"I knew that one," Stephanie said, smiling at his comment about her favorite game. "Anything else we should know?"

"Well, don't compliment someone on their pants," he said.

"Why not?" Jordan asked.

"Because pants are what they call underwear over there," Justin said.

"Nice pants, Justin," Stephanie said, giggling as Justin turned a deep shade of red.

An hour into the flight, Aimee brought trays with burgers and fries. While they were eating dinner, the four friends talked excitedly about their plans for the trip.

"I want to go on the London Eye," Jordan said.

"I want to go to Stonehenge," Catherine said.

"And we can't miss the changing of the guard at Buckingham Palace," Stephanie said.

"I want to see the Crown Jewels at the Tower of London," Justin added.

"There will be plenty of time for everything," Catherine's dad said as he walked up the aisle from the back of the jet where he and Justin's dad had been discussing their meeting plans.

"In the meantime, how about you get a little sleep so you'll be ready to go when we land?" Justin's dad said.

"Wait, we can't go to bed yet!" Jordan said.

"Why not? Is your head too full of ideas on what you want to do?" Justin's dad asked.

"No, my belly is too empty," Jordan responded. "Aimee promised us dessert."

"And I always keep my promises," Aimee said as she produced a tray of bowls heaped with ice cream. "Who's ready for ice cream?" She scooped hot fudge onto the ice cream and added whipped cream and a cherry on top.

After the hot fudge sundaes, the four kids reclined their seats to form beds. Aimee supplied pillows and blankets and dimmed the lights. Within minutes, the four had drifted off to sleep forty-one thousand feet over the Atlantic Ocean.

In the back of the plane, the two dads talked quietly. Justin's dad brought up BBC News on his laptop.

"Hmm, this doesn't look good," he said.

"What's that?"

"This news article says London is under a heightened security level due to suspected terrorist activity. Just

An Artificial Test

chatter so far, but the authorities are concerned," Justin's dad said.

"Well, since we'll be meeting with the folks from Scotland Yard, I'm sure we'll hear all about it."

"You think the kids will be okay on their own?"

"I'm sure they'll be in good hands with the guide we hired," Catherine's dad replied. "Besides, the kids have a good eye for trouble."

"That's what I'm worried about," Justin's dad said. "If there is trouble to be found, our kids seem to have a knack for finding it."

Acknowledgments

There is a quote often attributed to Antoine de Saint Exupéry (1900-1944), a French writer and aviator. It says that if you want to build a ship, you don't gather up people and assign them tasks. Instead, you should teach them to long for the vastness of the sea. The quote is not about building ships. It's about dreaming of a destination and letting that dream drive the journey. I'd argue it's also about math.

We learn about math from an early age, but these early lessons are...well, let's say they are less than exciting. We need to teach children that there is so much more to math—amazing patterns, incredible architecture, beautiful artwork, haunting music. We don't have to teach them why the math works (not yet anyway), but we need to let them know the destination is well worth the journey. The Math Kids is my attempt to start to paint this wonderful picture.

Thanks to Common Deer Press, Kirsten Marion for starting this journey, and to Emily Stewart for working so hard to get all the details right while also keeping me on schedule. Thanks, Emily, for being gentle with your criticism and relentless with getting it right.

Special thanks to Shannon O'Toole—the artwork is always great but working with you is even better. I owe you one for repainting an entire cover when I couldn't keep my own characters straight. You did it without complaint, and you nailed it as always.

To Stephanie, Jordan, and Justin, thanks for loving me despite my faults (while still managing to remind me of those faults when I need to hear it). To Debbie, it continues to be a journey I wouldn't want to take with anyone else.

As always, I want to thank my readers. You can contact me at TheMathKids.com. I love hearing from you!

About the Author

David Cole has always been passionate about math. His background is in math, mechanical engineering, and computer science, and he has done everything from designing missile guidance systems to teaching college computer science classes to designing data center management software. He has coached many different math teams, and he ran a summer math camp for elementary school students for a number of years. He found that one of the best ways to teach math was to do it through games and stories. Most campers were reluctant to give up a week of their summer to math, but after attending once, they kept coming back year after year. The Math Kids series was born from the stories David told to get kids to understand and actually like math. David is the author of the six previous books in the Math Kids series and is currently working on the next one. To keep up with the adventures of Stephanie, Justin, Jordan, and Catherine as they use their math skills to solve mysteries, deal with classroom bullies, and help their friends, check out TheMathKids.com.